A SHIFT
IN THE
EARTH

PATRICIA D. EDDY

PROLOGUE

FARREN

Where was she? It was dark, and she couldn't move. Her lips were parted, but when she tried to inhale, it was like breathing through a pinhole.

Her head ached, and it took her several seconds to realize her eyes weren't open. Her inability to breathe took precedence over everything else, and she focused on the smallest movements until her body started to spasm, and then a rush of oxygen flooded her lungs.

Two, three deep breaths, and then...nothing. Again. Fuck.

A slap stung her cheek, and she forced her eyes open. Dark hair. Wild, hazel eyes. And a smile that chilled her down to her bones. "About time ya' woke up. Now listen here. I need ya' to lie still. Ya' can do as I say, and I'll let ya' breathe, or I can take yer air and ya' can feel like ye're going to die the whole time. Yer choice."

After another wave of fresh air Farren gulped down, she managed, "I'll be...still."

She wouldn't. Not in the least. Because whatever this arse was planning, it wouldn't be pleasant. Not with the blade in his hand. But she'd be good for nothing if she couldn't breathe.

And how the hell was he doing that anyway? Taking all the air from the room? Fergus Tharp was an earth elemental. Not air. Her eyes adjusted to the dim light, and all around them, dirt walls. Shorn up by the occasional wooden beam. It smelled like the earth. Like wet soil, so they had to be underground somewhere.

He'd tied her wrists and then rolled her onto her back so her arms were pinned. Her legs were free, but as she tried to sense the muscles, they didn't respond.

Fuck. She could feel them, though.

"Did...ya'...drug me?" she gasped, still reeling from the near suffocation.

"I compelled ya'. Works kinda' like a drug, I suppose," he said as he yanked up her tank top to expose her stomach.

"What...? Please don't..." she said as she tried to wriggle away, but Fergus kicked her in the ribs and her breath left her again.

"I told ya' not to move. Warned ya', I did. Now ye're goin' to have to deal with the pain."

Dropping to one knee, he traced the tip of the blade against her side.

Farren's eyes watered, the lack of oxygen sending black spots pinging in her vision. Until Fergus snarled and pressed the knife harder, so hard it cut into her, burning a line from her bottom rib almost to her hip. Blood dripped along her side. She could feel each little rivulet, how it rolled along her skin and fell to the floor underneath her.

His hand shook, and he cursed viciously, muttered a few words her addled brain couldn't understand, and let her breathe. Stalking away, Fergus paced the room, continuing to talk to himself.

"I need my air. She's my air. And once I get her back..." He kicked the wall, whispering again, and Farren's world went dark and quiet as her entire body strained just to survive.

———

HER WOLF RAILED against the chains binding her. The beast couldn't understand why she was trapped—nor did Farren. How long had she been here? Two hours? Six? A full day?

It took her forever just to move her hand enough to feel for the wounds along her side. One long, deep slice. A shorter cut next to it.

Her stomach rumbled. Unsurprising as she and Colin hadn't eaten since noon. Where was her beta?

"Colin," she whispered, the single word strained and hoarse. "Where are ya'?"

Only silence answered her.

Until a door banged open and a dim light shone down on her from above. Fergus stomped over to her, grabbed her hair, and slammed her head into the ground.

"Ya' can't escape me, bitch."

The pocket knife snapped open, and he knelt next to her again, his hand shaking as he carved a third line into her skin. Farren screamed as best she could, still barely able to breathe, choking and trying to inch away from him. But there was too much blood. Her wolf howled deep inside, ready to spring and tear this fucking elemental limb from limb, but she couldn't shift.

"Please," she whimpered. "I've done...nothin' to ya'."

He slapped her across the face, and she tasted blood.

"Where's...Colin?"

"He's theirs now." Before Farren could ask what he meant and who *they* were, he flicked the knife in a half circle right over her ribs, and the wound burned like nothing she had ever felt.

Not like before. Not even like the time her wolf had fought her way out of a building consumed by flames.

What was happening to her? Her thoughts fuzzed, and it was like someone else was trying to force her to obey. To lie still. To accept this madman carving her up like she was his canvas.

"No!" Farren wailed, and Fergus jerked back, dropped the knife, and started to pace once more.

"My air. I need my air." He reached into his pocket for a bottle of pills, tossed three into his mouth, and crunched them like candy. "Ya' cannot fight them, wolf. I tried. Ya' need to help me now. Help me get my air."

"No." The word escaped on a snarl, and she kicked at him, but she was too weak, and he launched himself on top of her, punching and thrashing her until at least two ribs snapped and her forearm broke with a twisting pain that spiraled from her shoulder to her fingertips.

And all of a sudden, he stopped. Just...calmly rose, spun on a heel, and headed for the door. "Ya' need to understand. And ya' will."

The whole dark, dirty room shook, and Farren closed her eyes, reaching for her wolf.

Please. Fight. He can't keep ya' inside me forever.

She'd always talked to her beast. For as long as she could remember. Her mum had too. Even though her da' never understood why. She knew the animal could hear her. The sleek, white wolf was her best friend. Half of her soul, of her very existence. The only being who'd ever understood her.

The wolf howled, long and low, a desperate, feral sound, and tried to claw her way free. Farren's skin tingled. Just the faintest hint.

Yes. Keep going, ya' badass bitch. We're not just going to lie down and die. Ya' hear me?

The wolf fought harder, trying to tear Farren apart from the inside out. She welcomed the pain. Embraced it. The bastard would die. Because it was him or her, and there was no way she was leaving this world with some fucking symbol carved into her side.

And controlled by another? Fuck that.

Her skin started to burn, and her bones felt like they were about to crumble into dust. She let out a high-pitched scream, and her neck cracked. One vertebrae. Two. Three. Four.

Her clothes. She had to get out of her clothes.

I'm tryin'. I know it hurts.

The wolf whined, and Farren's legs shattered. Her fingernails sharpened into claws, and she sliced the ropes binding her wrists, then went to work on her black leather pants, tearing them at her hips until they were no more than shreds.

Finally freed, her wolf crawled towards the door. So weak from loss of blood. She needed to eat. Needed to sleep. Needed to get out of this fucking place.

The door wouldn't budge. But Farren started to dig. The earth was soft. Almost muddy. Easy for her beast to tear through with nails and paws and teeth. She spit out huge mouthfuls, the taste bitter. Imbued with some evil sort of magic Farren couldn't understand. Not in this form.

She could think. She had her human faculties. And would for at least a day or so. After that...if she couldn't shift back, her thoughts would dull. But not yet. Under the door would be easiest, and after less than an hour—she thought—she wriggled her lupine body beneath the metal frame.

Limping slowly up a set of stairs, she emerged into a cloudy night, no moon to light her way.

She had no idea where she was. Or how far she'd been taken from Lahinch or her home. Scenting the air, she tried to find Colin, but all she could smell were Fergus and the sea.

Her wolf started to run—if anyone could call what the animal was doing running—and she didn't stop until she simply couldn't push herself any longer.

A tall copse of cedar stood against the edge of the cliff, and Farren staggered over to it and slunk behind the large trunks. Her wolf collapsed, and she stared up at the branches swaying in the wind.

She'd done it. She'd escaped somehow. But her survival depended on her ability to hide—and keep moving—and she wasn't sure she could do either.

A twig snapped, and she jerked, tried to get up, and fell over again with a small whimper.

"Easy now." The man's raspy voice was familiar, and she tried to place it. To remember his name. "Old Paddy's here. He'll take care of ya'."

Paddy.

Doolin's oldest and most mysterious resident. The daft man spoke in riddles. Half the time, Farren was convinced his rational mind had fled decades ago. But still, she trusted him, though she couldn't explain why.

He picked his way over the uneven ground and crept towards her. Blanket. He had a blanket in his hands.

She might still have her wits about her, but her wolf was a creature of instinct, and right now, the animal was shivering and in pain. Blankets meant warmth. Comfort.

"Come with Paddy. He'll hide ya' till it's time for air to find ya'."

Farren crawled over to the man, and when he wrapped the blanket around her wolf's torso, she relaxed. He'd help her. He'd keep her safe.

ELI

As the sun set, the crowds dwindled until Eli was alone on the beach save for a young man on a surfboard trying to catch that one perfect wave.

For a full hundred meters, a massive phoenix graced the sand, its wings spread in flight with flames dripping from its tail. He wasn't sure why he'd felt so compelled to create the mythical bird out of hard packed sand using only his hands and the bare minimum of tools, but then again, he never knew what form his sculptures would take until they were complete.

The hours he spent working? He had little to no memory of them. Every time. He created until his muscles ached and his hands were blistered and raw. Until something inside him let him know he was done.

The tide had already started to rise, and he dug his fingers into the sand until he touched the tip of the magnificent bird's beak, marring his creation and freeing him from whatever hold the artwork had over him.

Knowing all his work would be washed away overnight didn't sadden him. If anything, it gave him hope.

Tomorrow, the beach would be someone else's fresh canvas. A new start. A clean slate.

He'd been lucky. No one had come to stop him. These random, unplanned demonstrations of his artistic talents weren't licensed or sanctioned by the government, and he knew he risked arrest. But when he was between sculpting projects, he often felt the need to "play in the sand," as his last girlfriend had once called it.

Tipping the bucket next to him, he let out a low whistle. He'd collected over a thousand euros today. Passersby would often drop coins or bills for him as they watched his creations come to life—a little extra if he offered to sculpt their likenesses off to the side of his "canvas."

Today, he'd worked his magic to create an image of an entire family. Mother, father, two daughters, and a son. The youngest child—a girl—had been so enthralled by seeing him draw her mother's likeness in the sand that she'd clapped and giggled the whole time. And then the father had dropped a fat wad of bills into the bucket.

The waves crested twenty meters away, and the very end of the phoenix tail disappeared—lost to the sea. The lone surfer paddled back out over the breaking surf, and Eli peered up at the horizon. Black clouds were rolling in, and the wind had started to howl. Or warn.

Get back to the beach, you dolt.

The kid toppled off his board, then got right back up, heading out to catch his perfect wave again and again, and by the time Eli had finished packing up his tools, the rain soaked his jet black hair. His phoenix was no more, and he checked all around him. Not a single soul graced the shrinking strip of sand. He couldn't just leave. Not with the surfer still out there.

He approached the high water mark and started waving his arms at the young man, signaling him to come in. Finally, the guy nodded, but then cast a quick glance behind him.

"No!" Eli shouted. The wave had to be at least twenty meters tall, and the surfer started to spiral his arms frantically, trying to outrun what could never, *ever* be beaten. The kid didn't have a chance.

Churning white water pulled man and board under, and Eli stood, his feet rooted to the sand. He could do nothing but watch as the ocean came for him, and when the rush of the inflow knocked him head over heels, he tasted the sea, choked on it, and fought its pull.

He didn't know which way was up. The water stole everything from him. His view of the sky. His voice. Even his sense of time. His heartbeat roared in his ears, and he wondered if this was how he'd die.

No. Not like this. Please.

He didn't know if there was an afterlife. His boarding school education and his time at university had both included religious studies, but he'd never really thought about whether he...*believed*.

But now...he prayed. Prayed to every deity he could think of as his life flashed before his eyes. His very boring, very lonely life.

When his head broke through the surface, he spit out a mouthful of brackish water. Fuck. He had to be at least fifty meters from shore, and as he tried to stay afloat, he caught sight of the surfer. The guy was face down, and Eli fought against the current, desperate to reach him.

Flipping the guy over, he battled his panic. The young man couldn't be more than twenty, and his lips were blue. Eli's muscles were starting to lock up from the cold. The waters off the far northeastern shore of England weren't ones you messed with. Or ever tried to swim in without a wetsuit.

He got his arm around the surfer and started kicking with everything he had left. Yet whenever he looked up to sight the beach, they seemed to be farther and farther away.

"No! Not like this! I want to live!" he screamed into the gale.

Despite the ocean's unrelenting chaos, Eli thought he felt the earth start to shake. A great rumble surrounded him, and the water churned even more violently, the spray stinging his cheeks and making his eyes tear up.

His foot hit something that shouldn't be there. It almost felt like...land? Kicking even harder, his toes scraped against rocks. When had he lost his shoes? He had no idea. But after another few seconds, he was standing.

All around him, the water receded, leaving a path of rocks and sand that led to the beach. The waves grew angrier the longer he stood, afraid to move, as if they were railing against invisible walls keeping them away.

Move.

The voice was his own, even though he hadn't spoken. One step. Two. Three. And then, with the surfer slung over his shoulder, Eli started to run and didn't stop until he was at least ten meters from the high water line. His strength gave out, and he collapsed onto the sand.

The waves, suddenly set free, rushed into shore, but somehow, Eli knew they'd never reach him. A cough, the surfer forcing the water from his lungs, drew his focus, and he slapped the kid on the back a few times, hoping that was what one was supposed to do for someone who'd almost drowned.

"What…what happened?" the kid asked, his wide eyes bloodshot as he stared out into the quickly darkening waters.

"I have no fucking clue."

CHAPTER ONE

FARREN

ea in hand, she trudged out to the back porch. Barely dawn, but this was the time of day she loved most. When everything was quiet and fresh and new. No fussing from Tierney or Ewan—the only two members of her pack she had left. No moans of pleasure coming from upstairs where Liam and Caitlin were still enjoying the first passionate months of their mating. No retching from Mara, Cade's elemental mate, who was now—they estimated—more than four months pregnant.

The morning mists let her pretend she hadn't lost everything. Hadn't gotten two—if not three—members of her pack killed. For all she knew Abagail was still alive somewhere, but the young female wolf hadn't contacted her since disappearing weeks ago.

Out here, she could forget that she'd almost lost Liam—the man who was like a brother to her—or that she hadn't helped *kill* an earth elemental who'd come after them, torturing her, leaving her with a scar that a dozen shifts couldn't heal.

The waxing moon sank below the horizon, and the intense pull to shift, to run, to let her wolf free started to abate.

At the tree line, the bushes rustled, and a moment later, Tierney's dark brown wolf padded across the expanse of lawn. Dropping down next to Farren's chair, he whined as his bones started to pop and crack, his fur rippled, and his snout shortened into a human nose.

The entire shift took less than a minute, and when he lay naked and panting on the flagstones, Farren reached over to the adjacent chair, snagged a black robe, and dropped it next to him.

"Watch it, young one. That pale arse could blind someone this early in the mornin'."

"Like ya' have any room to talk. Ye're paler than I am." Tierney shoved his arms into the robe, staggered upright long enough to tie the belt, and then took a seat in the chair next to her.

Farren snorted. "That I may be, but I leave my clothes in the woods."

"Too many pine needles. And bugs."

She arched her brows. City boy. Fastidious. Almost to a fault. A rule follower. But he meant well, and he and Ewan were loyal. Too loyal, in fact.

"What?" he asked. "Ya' want a beetle crawling up yer crack?" Shrugging, he shook his head. "Suit yerself."

Her laugh felt strange. Like she didn't have any right to that particular light-hearted emotion. Not now. Not after everything that had happened. But there was also normalcy to it, and she couldn't decide how she felt about that.

"Is anyone else up?" Tierney asked.

"No. Or at least, no one's come downstairs." Turning to the boy, she held his earnest gaze. "Are ya' sure ya' don't want to head to Shannon and join up with that football league for a spell? You and Ewan could see more of the world. I hear they're goin' all the way to Scotland for their openin' match."

"Are ya' orderin' me to go?" The words rumbled through Tierney's chest with a hard edge, and he quickly stared down at his hands in his lap. "As my alpha?"

Blowing out a breath, Farren shook her head. "No. Of course not. But—"

"Then stop mentionin' it. I'm stayin'." He lumbered to his feet, his six-foot-four inch frame towering over her, yet he still managed to look submissive. That's what he was, after all. At least to her. He wasn't born to lead. Hell, he'd refused to even consider taking over as her beta. He was smart enough. Loved his wolf. Loved life itself.

"Farren," he said quietly, "ye're my alpha. I pledged my loyalty to ya' years ago, and not a thing has changed. If ye'll excuse me, I'm gonna catch a couple a' hours before I get back to helpin' Caitlin with that book of hers. Every time we try to make it past the fifth page, the letters..." He shook his head and a shock of dark brown hair fell into his eyes. "They change. Spelled. We even tried takin' pictures, but whatever magic Diedre used...it's powerful. Affects the photos too."

"Fuckin' magic," Farren muttered. "Not a single good thing ever came from a practitioner."

"Ya' can't mean that. The sigils Caitlin used at the cliffs...they saved all of us. And what about Paddy?"

With a sigh, Farren carded her fingers through her silvery blond hair. "Paddy's the exception. Barely. All those damn riddles. I can't decide if I want to strangle the man or hug him half the time." With a quick glance back towards the house, she nodded. "Go on up, then. Get some rest. And don't say a word about—"

"About ya' tryin' to send us away? Don't worry. I won't." The door slammed behind him, and Farren winced. If she weren't careful, she'd soon say something she'd regret. Something she couldn't take back.

Like how she was a rubbish alpha. How she wished she could just escape. Run away from all of her responsibilities and be...free.

For more than ten years, she'd led her pack with Colin at her side. They'd grown up together. Her and Colin and Liam. Thick as thieves, always getting into trouble. The pressure of being one of the only female alphas in the world hadn't felt so terrible when she'd been able to lean on the beta wolf.

But Colin was gone now. Tortured, branded, and eventually killed by Fergus, the earth elemental who'd tried to steal Caitlin's air away at the behest of the Thirteen—a group of the most powerful practitioners in the world.

Every time Farren closed her eyes, she saw his broken body. Heard his final scream as Fergus had brought down a building to get to them.

Her eyes started to burn. Setting down her tea, she slapped her leg hard enough to leave a bruise. The physical pain drew her focus, and she could breathe again.

If she did manage to drive Tierney and Ewan away, would that be a blessing? At least then, she wouldn't have to look her failure in the eyes every day.

She knew the boy, though. He wouldn't leave. Neither of them would. They'd just start to resent her and she resented herself enough for all of them.

Footsteps thudded on the stairs. Liam, from the sound. And if Liam were up, Cade would soon follow. Along with their mates.

The small amount of peace Farren had found out here in the mists would have to last her until tomorrow. She might not feel up to leading a pack anymore, but she could at least make breakfast.

"GET BACK HERE!" Farren called as Liam grabbed Caitlin around the waist and threw her over his shoulder. "Ya' could at least help with the dishes, ya' arse!"

"Later," Liam growled as he carried his mate up the stairs.

Shaking her head, Farren took one look at the table filled with empty plates, crumpled napkins, and crumbs leftover from tall stacks of pancakes and at least five kilos of bacon. With Cade, Liam, and Peter here, along with their mates, her grocery bill had doubled.

"We'll take care of it," Tierney said as he started piling the dishes in a tower Farren knew was a *very* bad idea. But somehow, the young wolf made it all the way to the sink with ease. He was a miracle, that one. And the only one of the lot she could take credit for.

Ewan had come to her only two years ago. But Tierney...he'd been with her for almost a decade. Ever since his father had turned him out for being "a monster." His mother had been a wolf, but she'd hidden it from his father for Tierney's whole life until the boy was fourteen and shifted for the first time.

If it weren't for Tierney, would she still even be here? In this house? Leading—or pretending to lead—what remained of her pack? Probably not.

The sounds of Liam and Caitlin laughing—and doing other things—carried as Farren climbed the stairs. She had to get away from this disgusting love-fest that had taken over her second floor. With two newly mated couples, someone was getting lucky in her house almost every hour of the day. And it was never her.

Racing to the top floor as quickly as she could, Farren changed into a pair of black leather pants, an emerald green sweater, and her heaviest boots. Running a brush through her silvery locks, she scowled as she caught tangle after tangle.

Her mother would lecture her. She hadn't been taking care of herself for weeks now.

Not that she was high maintenance. But before this whole mess had started, she'd at least managed the basics. Fifty strokes of the brush every night before bed. A warm bath after each shift to relax her muscles. A decent amount of sleep.

Now, she spent her nights running to escape the stress. Caitlin and Tierney had translated enough of the old practitioner's book of magic to believe that Mara, whose fire elemental powers were still causing her to lose time, would be whole again once she gave birth. But that wouldn't happen for another twelve weeks—at least.

Werewolves only carried their young for seven months, and no one knew exactly how long an elemental's pregnancy would be, but at—give or take—fourteen weeks, Mara already had a significant baby bump and she'd started to feel the pup kick. If they could just get through the next three months, maybe life would return to normal.

Oh, who was she kidding? The Thirteen had put a target on Mara's back the moment she'd killed her sister and absorbed Katerina's fire element. If they could get their hands on her, they'd be halfway to their goal of channeling all four elements into a single person to make the fifth element—spirit. And if that happened...not even God herself could save the world from magic.

Farren gave up on her hair and pulled the long strands into a ponytail. It'd be easier to tuck into her motorcycle helmet that way. She needed to feel the road. To feel...free. Hell, if she could shift and run all the way to her office in town, she would. But she didn't have any spare clothes waiting for her, and working naked wasn't the best way to attract a legitimate client.

Now to get out of the house without anyone seeing her—or stopping her.

CHAPTER TWO

ELI

Twenty minutes. If he could keep it together for another twenty minutes, he'd be on the ground and this terrible nausea would fade.

He'd downed four shots of expensive whiskey at one of the airport pubs before he got on the plane, and thank God the flight was only a little over an hour. That much alcohol was dangerous, he knew, but it was either that or pass the flight in the tiny lavatory, huddled on the floor, alternately throwing up and fading into unconsciousness.

At least he'd warned the flight attendants of his past terrible experiences on planes. When he'd gone to Hawaii five years ago, completely unaware of how badly he'd react to flying, they'd broken into the lavatory and dragged him out of there less than an hour after takeoff. The pilot had turned the plane around, and he'd spent a rather uncomfortable afternoon with security at Gatwick, trying to explain what he couldn't understand himself. How he'd been perfectly fine until the plane had reached cruising altitude, and then totally lost his shit.

This flight hadn't been quite as terrible as he'd feared. He'd almost broken down and booked a car ferry instead, but after nearly drowning less than two weeks ago, being on the water was even less appealing than taking to the air.

Ireland was visible out the window—had been most of the flight—and the sight of land made him feel marginally better. He still had at least a three hour drive ahead of him—once he sobered up—but he'd be in Doolin by late afternoon, and maybe then he'd find some answers.

Scoffing at his own stupidity, he let his head fall back against the seat. What was he doing? Flying—something he hated—to a country he'd never seen all because some daft old woman in a Greenwich pub had told him he'd find answers there. And protection.

What the fuck did he need protection from?

From the bastards who broke in to your flat and probably would have killed you had you not noticed the busted lock.

Three men and one woman had been waiting for him to come home, but all of them managed to evade capture. The police had been as baffled as he was. Though he made a good living selling his sculptures and performing semi-regular displays of his sand art, he lived simply, choosing to invest most of his earnings rather than spend them.

The criminals had taken nothing but his birth certificate. After filing all of the appropriate forms to protect his identity and credit, he'd tried to forget about the violation. About strangers in his private space. But something about the scent that permeated the entire flat made him physically ill every time he entered, and eventually, he'd packed a bag and moved to a hotel.

That's where he'd met the strange woman. Snow white hair, wrinkled skin, purple eyes, and a voice that haunted his dreams.

"Doolin is where ya' must go. Ye're not safe here. Not anywhere. Not without protection. Find the silver wolf, and when the time is right, she'll know what to do."

And then the woman had pressed a small pouch into his hand. He'd been so fixated on it, on the feel of the velvety bag, on the way it sat heavy in his palm, that he hadn't seen her slip away into the crowd.

As the pilot welcomed them to Dublin, Eli reached into his pocket, making sure the bag was still there. Inside lay a silver pendant with an intricate design—the tree of life made up of Celtic trinity knots. When he touched it, he could almost believe it was a living, breathing *thing*, and not merely a piece of jewelry.

He'd never believed in magic. In the *other*. Yet here he was, on Irish soil, about to hunt down a silver wolf? He just hoped Doolin had a zoo and the old woman hadn't intended for him to track down a wild animal—one that could easily kill him.

NOT LONG BEFORE SUNDOWN, he slowed his rented sports car as he entered Doolin. He'd thought it a town, but it was little more than a cluster of buildings around one main street.

Eli counted three pubs, one still under construction, a boarding house that couldn't possibly have more than six rooms, a grocery store, and a petrol station.

This was where he was supposed to find a silver wolf? Hardly. He'd be lucky to find a decent pint and some chips.

Why had he listened to the old woman?

Because nothing in your life at the moment makes sense, so why not?

His inner voice needed to shut the hell up, but since when had it ever behaved? He'd ended up in the headmaster's office regularly back in boarding school because of it—and his habit of repeating whatever it said out loud.

But it had saved his life when he'd been about to drown. And stopped him from barging right into his flat after seeing the busted lock. So he'd trust it now. For at least a little longer.

Unsure where to start, he parked along a side street and headed for the largest pub. The weathered wooden sign proclaimed it *O'Connor's Pub*, and next to the hand-carved letters was a rough likeness of a wolf.

"Fuck me, this is too much," he muttered. But he'd come this far. Might as well see if fate—or whatever was guiding him these days—wanted to offer him another breadcrumb to follow.

Inside, a small band played in one corner, but only half of the tables were occupied, and the bartender chatted with a burly man on one of the stools. Eli's stomach growled as the scent of chips and something richer—a stew, perhaps—wafted towards him. If all he got out of this place was a hearty meal and a pint, he'd count himself lucky.

"What'll it be, mate?" the bartender asked when Eli slid into one of the empty seats.

"Got a local ale on tap?"

"Donegal Blonde and the Dooliner Irish Red. I'd favor the Red."

The man nodded approvingly when Eli took him up on his suggestion, poured the pint, and gestured to a chalkboard on the wall for the menu.

After ordering a bowl of Guinness stew with a side of chips, Eli turned his attention to the band. They had an easy rapport with one another, the fiddle player telling jokes between songs, and a girl who couldn't be more than fifteen working the concertina like a master.

"Ye're new to Doolin, yeah?" the bartender asked as he delivered Eli's meal.

"Just passing through. I think." Staring into his stew, he

muttered, "Unless this town has a petting zoo with a silver wolf."

Eli expected the man to give him the side eye. Or maybe to chuckle. Not to stagger back against the counter laughing so hard tears brimmed in his eyes.

"Oh, ya' want Farren, mate. But if ya' ever dare tell her ya' thought she'd be in a pettin' zoo, ye'll regret the day ya' were born." Pulling a handkerchief from his pocket, he dabbed his eyes and shook his head. "Pettin' zoo. Ya' *definitely* aren't from around these parts."

"London." When the bartender didn't offer up any additional explanation, Eli sat up a little straighter. "I don't suppose you could tell me where I can find this...Farren?"

"Two blocks south. Ya' can't miss the sign." Still chuckling to himself, the bartender grabbed the bill he'd set next to Eli's beer. "On the house. If Farren don't eat ya' alive, ya' can come back and settle up later. A man shouldn't pay for his last meal."

Great. He'd found his silver wolf who wasn't a wolf at all but a woman. And now a man he'd never met before automatically assumed he couldn't hold his own? Fucking idiot.

After he drained the last of his pint, he dug into his pocket and withdrew a twenty euro note. No matter how rude the bloke had been, he wasn't going to walk out without at least a tip.

He'd be back in an hour—or less—and pay his bill in full.

FARREN

Her dark green office walls always settled her mind. As did the quiet. Most of her cases came to her by email—or by word of mouth when she'd wander down to O'Connor's for lunch or a pint if she wanted to avoid returning to the chaos of her current home life.

Just that morning, Cade had found Mara wandering down the rocky driveway, barefoot, wearing only a tank top and loose fleece pants. The yelling and cursing that had filled her main room after that...her head still ached.

Mara's episodes were getting worse. Lasting longer. Months ago, the poor woman had killed her own sister in order to save Cade and the rest of the pack. In doing so, she'd absorbed Katerina's fire, and now...it was killing her. Two elements couldn't coexist without driving the bearer mad.

For some, like Fergus, the earth elemental who'd come after Caitlin and given Farren the scar on her side that would never fade, the madness was near constant, but Mara's struggles were almost more dangerous. When her fire element asserted itself, her mind...

"It's like I'm locked in this tiny box with no control over anything. I can see and hear. And that's the worst part, Farren. I know what the fire is making me do. But I'm powerless to stop it."

One of the only times they'd spoken of Mara's episodes, the water elemental had ended up crying in Farren's arms, and wasn't that just the most awkward thing? If she were more like Caitlin, she'd have been able to comfort Mara. Liam's mate could make anyone feel safe and protected.

Farren didn't have a comforting or motherly bone in her entire body. She was an alpha, head to toe, nose to tail, and she didn't hold with softness. She could pretend for a short while, and she would. Whenever Mara was around. She'd do it for Cade. For Liam and Caitlin. Not that it did any good.

The last incident Farren had witnessed before this morning? Mara had been so far gone, she'd almost set fire to the bedroom she and Cade shared on the second floor. If not for Caitlin's quick work depriving the flames of oxygen, the whole house could have gone up.

And if Mara had made it any farther this morning, she would have escaped the wards that Paddy and the old practitioner, Diedre, had set to hide Mara's power from the Thirteen.

For six weeks, those wards had kept them safe. But they had also kept the elementals trapped on Farren's property, and everyone was going a bit stir crazy.

Shite. She just needed to escape for a few days. Find some case to dig her teeth into. Perhaps literally.

Scanning her email for the tenth time that afternoon, she blew out a long breath. Empty. At this point, she'd take anything. Even a scorned wife looking to tail her cheating husband. A lost cat. Misplaced car keys.

When folks learned she worked as a private investigator, they assumed she skulked around at night, dodged danger at every turn, and lived a life of excitement and intrigue. In reality, she spent most of her time hunting for information on the internet. Fergus Tharp had been the only danger she'd faced in three years.

Farren leaned back in her chair and stared out her tiny window. If she couldn't find a client soon, she'd go back home, hide upstairs until the moon rose, then shift and run until she couldn't run any further. It was either that or find a drink and a fight.

THOUGH HER FRONT window was heavily tinted to keep prying eyes from seeing in, Farren knew the moment the sun descended below the horizon. She couldn't put it off any longer and reached for her phone. If Caitlin needed anything for dinner, she could stop at the store. But two numbers into dialing, her office door opened.

"I'm looking for a woman named Farren?"

The tall, bronze-skinned god standing in front of her made

her jaw drop and her mouth go as dry as the Sahara in the space of a single breath. Unruly shocks of dark hair fell across his forehead, and pale green eyes, reminiscent of the sea after a storm, took her in. His full lips pursed briefly, and she let her gaze trail lower, across broad shoulders, corded arms, and a narrow waist and hips.

"I'm Farren Denair. Can I help ya'?" She stood and held out her hand. As his fingers brushed hers, a spark of electricity raced up her arm, and his scent, something rich with a hint of spice, made her core clench. It had been far too long since she'd been with a man, and this one ticked all her boxes.

"Eli Escobar." His accent was decidedly British, but colored with a bit of Ireland as well. "I...was sent here."

"Sent here? By whom?" Word-of-mouth cases held promise that she wouldn't have to hide her true nature, but something in Eli's eyes made her think the world of the *other* wasn't one he dabbled in regularly.

"This is going to sound like I'm off my rocker," he muttered. "And I probably am. But I found myself in a pub in Greenwich a few days ago after some...*trouble,* and this little old woman with white hair and deep purple eyes told me I had to go to Doolin and find the silver wolf. The bartender up the street said *you* were the silver wolf."

Fuck. The only woman Farren knew with purple eyes was the practitioner. Diedre. "What did this 'little old woman' look like? As many details as you can remember."

Eli's brows furrowed. "I'm afraid that's all I can tell you about her, Ms. Denair. That night is a bit of a blur for me. It's not every day I come home to find three people have broken into my flat. Or that someone I meet in a pub suggests I leave the country in search of an animal. If you don't mind my asking, why do they call you the silver wolf?"

Farren waved towards her visitor's chair and slipped back behind her desk when he took a seat. "Ya' don't know, then."

"Know?"

She studied the man across from her. Half of Doolin knew about werewolves. Practitioners. Elementals, even. Still, she'd be a complete idiot to simply *volunteer* her unique genetic makeup. He could be a member of the Thirteen or one of their minions.

"Have ya' ever seen somethin' ya' couldn't explain?"

"If you had asked me that six months ago, I would have said no. But now? Bloody hell. My entire life makes no sense these days." Weariness infused his tone, and he sat back in the chair and ran a hand through those messy locks.

Farren inhaled deeply, scenting him like her mother had taught her. For more than twenty years, her mum had been an inspector with the Garda, using her enhanced senses to determine when suspects were lying. "If ya' want me to enlighten ya'," she said as she rose and dragged her chair around the desk, "ya' need to face me and give me yer hands."

"This was a bloody stupid idea," Eli muttered. "What are you planning on doing? Reading my palms? My aura? I'm looking for answers, Ms. Denair. Not magic."

Farren rolled her eyes. "I can tell when people lie to me, *Mr.* Escobar. A gift, if ya' want to call it that. A talent. But not magic. Now give me yer hands."

They were rough. Calloused. Like he worked with them every day.

"What do ya' do for a livin'?" She almost lost herself to those green eyes. Mesmerizing wasn't strong enough of a word. Nor was green. Storms raged in those eyes.

"I'm an artist. Stone, clay, sand…"

"And that pays the bills?"

He jerked his hands away. "I don't see how that is any of your business. I can certainly pay your fee, Ms. Denair. Should I decide to hire you."

Farren almost regretted baiting him, but she needed a baseline. A way to tell true outrage from a lie. "Do you have any knowledge of magic?" she asked.

"Fuck me. No. Magic is a myth."

Truth. At least he thinks it is.

She wasn't going to waste any more of his time—or hers—if she didn't have to. He was pleasant to look at, and she found herself leaning closer without any reason to do so. Warning bells were going off in her head, so loud, she could no longer hear his heartbeat.

Get it together. Focus. This is yer first potential client in six weeks, and ye're letting yer hormones make all the decisions for ya! Mum would be so disappointed.

"Ms. Denair? Farren? Where is this going? I've been awake for almost thirty-six hours, and all I want is to get a room and sleep. And understand what's happening to my life."

Eli Escobar was an honest man. His entire *being* vibrated it. Earnest, wholesome, complete honesty. Also, desperation.

"They don't *call* me the silver wolf, Mr. Escobar." Farren braced herself, unsure how he'd take her next words. "I *am* the silver wolf. The silver *were*wolf."

CHAPTER THREE

ELI

A werewolf? He jerked out of the chair so quickly, it toppled over with a crash. "You're...a... No. This was a mistake. I'm sorry for bothering you."

He'd never moved so fast in his entire life as he did bolting from Farren's office and heading for his car. The woman—the werewolf?—called his name, but he ignored her until he'd locked the door and gunned the engine. Where the hell did he think he was going? It was dark outside, and the drive to get here had been perilous the last half an hour. Roads so narrow they were practically just suggestions carved into the landscape with thorny bushes encroaching on either side ready to reach out and swallow him and the sports car whole.

He'd need to get a room for the night and head back to Dublin in the morning.

Farren held up her hand as he sped past her, but he quickly turned onto the main road in search of one of the boarding houses he'd seen upon his arrival.

The second one had a single room available, and he handed over his credit card, signed the register, and headed directly for the tiny pub attached to the place.

Two hours later, after spending more on whiskey than he had on the flight from London, he staggered up the stairs, his vision blurry and his stomach protesting every movement. He'd regret this. Probably within the hour. But fuck. He couldn't possibly fall asleep with Farren's words rattling around in his head all night.

"I am the silver wolf. The silver werewolf."

Werewolves weren't real. The woman was as daft as the old crone in the Greenwich pub. And he'd wasted his time coming here. First thing in the morning, he'd head for the airport and be home—or at least at a hotel in London—by late afternoon.

The dreams came for him moments after he lay down, fully clothed save for his shoes. Almost drowning. The way the ocean had shuddered, sand and rocks forming a bridge underneath him, keeping the waves at bay until he and the surfer had been safely to shore.

He felt the same rumbling now. All around him. Not as strong, but just as shocking. Eli pushed up on an elbow and blinked hard. He'd failed to turn off any of the lights, and the one hanging from the ceiling was swinging back and forth, the tray on the dresser with glasses and an ice bucket rattled.

Earthquake.

A mild one, but he didn't think Ireland had many quakes. Then again, he'd seen the news reports a couple of months back. Several meters of the Cliffs of Moher had been completely destroyed by tremors unlike the country had ever seen.

"It's the end of the bloody world," he muttered. His stomach pitched, and the shaking stopped abruptly. Thank God or he wouldn't have made it to the bathroom before he heaved up the liquor and the remaining contents of his stomach.

Never drinking like that again.

He rested his back against the wall, letting the cool plaster wash away the last vestiges of the nightmare.

Only to have the horrible images replaced by memories of Farren. Her eyes. The softness of her hands as she'd taken his. The musical lilt to her voice and the way her smile had stirred something inside of him he'd never felt before. A longing. A base need as strong as breathing.

Mostly sober, though with a headache that threatened to split his skull in half, he climbed back into bed and pulled out his phone.

Did one simply search the internet for werewolves? It seemed like the best place to start. Though most of the results led him to romance novels or video game characters.

The rest... A Wikipedia entry with references to the origin of the "werewolf mythos" and links to famous werewolves in historical fiction and lore.

Unwilling to risk sleep, he kept going. Pages and pages of results. Eventually, he admitted defeat and set the phone on the nightstand, closing his eyes and hoping this time, the dreams would stay far, far away.

FARREN

She'd run half the night away, and still tossed and turned for the few hours she tried to sleep, unable to forget Eli's eyes. His scent. The way he'd moved. The feel of his hands on hers.

Something about him made her all warm and soft in places she'd never been warm and soft before. She had a healthy stock of batteries and a couple of toys in her nightstand that took care of her needs when she was desperate, but even those hadn't worked to help her sleep.

It hadn't been hard to track Eli down. There were only eighteen hotel rooms in Doolin spread among three establishments. His scent lingered at Doolin House, and she'd stood outside the window of the hotel's small pub and watched him drink himself into oblivion.

She'd spooked him. No. Scratch that. She'd scared the piss out of him. At least she knew he wasn't a practitioner. Or an elemental.

Morning dawned clear and cool, and she was shocked to find Liam pouring himself a cup of coffee when she padded downstairs. "What are ya' doin' up so early?" she asked as she grabbed a mug for herself.

"Mara had another episode a few hours ago. Caitlin's been up with her since four. She's gettin' worse. I don't know how much more Cade can take."

Farren moved to the living room and sank down onto one of the leather couches. Tierney and Caitlin had left half a dozen pages of transcribed sigils scattered over the dark wood table in front of the hearth, and she picked one up, staring at letters and symbols that made no sense to her.

"There has to be a better way than this. I haven't seen Paddy in town in weeks, and without him, we'll never find Diedre again."

Unless she went back and talked to Eli. While there was no guarantee the woman he'd met in that Greenwich pub had been the practitioner they'd been looking for, it was their only lead.

"What is it?" Liam stood in front of her, his eyes narrowed. "Ye're on to somethin'. Tell me. I've never seen Cade this close to losin' control. He's an alpha to his core—just like you—and he can't stand seein' his mate in pain."

Just like me.

If only she *wasn't* an alpha. Then she could confide in her oldest friend. Tell him how very little she felt like a leader these days. How she'd gotten Colin and Brian killed. How she wished she could simply run away and never look back.

With a sigh, she drained the mug and returned to the kitchen for a refill. Caffeine didn't affect werewolves for very long—their fast metabolism burned it off like water, but the taste still helped her focus. If she was going to have a conversation with Eli Escobar, she was going to need every one of her wits about her.

"A new client came to see me last night," she said quietly when Liam stalked after her and growled her name. "Ended up boltin' the moment he found out I was a wolf."

"What the fuck did ya' tell him for?" Slamming his own cup down on the counter, Liam started to reach for Farren, probably to grab her by the shoulders and shake her, but then jerked away suddenly.

Newly mated werewolves were territorial and possessive, but the emotions ran both ways. Not only would Liam not stand for any other male—wolf or not—touching his Caitlin, he wouldn't willingly put his hands on another woman ever again.

As she tried not to chuckle at his reaction, she idly wondered what would happen with two mated wolves of the same sex. Ewan's brother was gay. And mated. Maybe one day she'd ask him.

With a quick shake of her head, she refocused on Liam. "I told him because he said he'd been sent to find the silver wolf by a daft old woman who showed up at a pub in London."

"Diedre."

"Possibly. Or someone pullin' one over on him. He didn't know anythin' about our world. I made sure of that. But he also didn't strike me as naive. More...baffled at why he'd listened to the woman in the first place."

Eli had needed answers. If only she hadn't scared him off before she figured out the questions.

"So? Are ya' goin' after him?"

Before Farren could answer, Caitlin shuffled into the kitchen. "Is that coffee? Can I have some? Or the whole pot?"

She yawned and fitted herself to Liam's side. "Mara's sleeping. Finally. I had to charm her. About a dozen times. That baby does *not* like its mother being forced to do *anything.*"

"The *baby* is fighting you?" Farren asked. "How do you know?

Sighing as Liam pressed a cup into her hand, she met Farren's gaze. "I didn't realize how much Katerina taught me about auras and energy. She never let me use those skills, so I assumed I couldn't." After a sip of coffee, she shook her head slightly. "I was wrong. When I help Mara—give her some of my air to bolster her water—I can feel another presence pushing back at me. The baby...she's all fire."

"She?" Liam stared down at his mate in disbelief. "Ya' can tell it's a girl?"

"I can't be certain." A small smile curved Caitlin's lips. "But I think so."

Farren let her gaze rove over the expanse of forest behind the house. "And will she be a wolf too?"

"With Cade as her father?" Liam snorted. "He's the purest blood of all of us."

Liam was right. Farren had never seen anyone—man or woman—stronger than Cade. When he shifted, his wolf stood taller and prouder than the rest of his pack, and only she could match him for speed when they ran.

The whole idea of a child, though...of having one. Of wanting one... She feared she simply hadn't been born with that gene. Almost like being an alpha. This pack...what was left of it anyway...she'd fallen into leading them. It had been more Colin's idea than her own.

"Ya' need yer own pack, Farren. Yer da' won't kick ya' out, but he raised ya' to be an alpha. We could head to the coast. There are a handful of wolves near Doolin lookin' for a leader."

"Farren? Did ya' hear me?" Liam asked.

"Sorry." She blinked hard. "Long night. What did ya' say?"

Caitlin reached over and snagged Farren's hand, squeezing her fingers briefly. The contact wasn't totally unwelcome, but definitely unexpected. "Ya' need to relax, luv. When was the last time ya' slept through the night?"

She couldn't remember. A month? Two? Not since she'd heard about the return of Fergus Tharp. "It's not important. Are ya' sure Mara's stable enough to be alone?"

Deflect. Defer. Distract. Ever since she'd lost Colin and Brian, that was how she got through her days. And she'd keep doing all of those things until Cade's pack went home. Assuming they ever went home. Shite. What if they had to stay here under the protection spell forever? What if they never found a way to permanently hide from the Thirteen? Or keep Mara safe?

Caitlin was talking again. Farren needed to get her head on straight. Now.

"I'll know when she wakes up," the air elemental said. Her mate rubbed her shoulders, and Caitlin sighed. "Plus, Cade should be back soon."

As if the alpha wolf had heard Caitlin, he strode out of the woods, buck arse naked and unashamed, his lips set in a near-permanent scowl.

"How is she?" he asked.

Caitlin turned away, her cheeks flushing pink as Liam growled. "Put some damn clothes on."

As a general rule, wolves didn't care about being naked. Farren shifted with her pack every full moon, and often times in between. Without the presence of a mating bond, the sight of another's sky-clad body didn't do a feckin' thing for any of them. Outside of an academic appreciation.

Cade was all coiled muscles, always looking like he was about to snap at a moment's notice. Until he turned away to pull on his jeans. Dozens of scars crossed his shoulder blades and back. Burns from the months he'd spent trapped as his wolf by

Mara's sister, Katerina. The fire elemental had repeatedly tortured him by tossing rotten meat onto a patch of dirt so hot, it seared his skin and his paw pads whenever he tried to touch it. She'd kept him from shifting for so long, when Mara finally broke the charm, he couldn't speak or move. She'd cared for him, fed him, helped him remember who he was, all without knowing he'd claimed her as his.

"Better?" he asked, hands on his hips. "How. Is. Mara?"

"She's resting. But tonight..." Caitlin looked from Liam to Farren and back to Cade. "I think we need to get her out into the backyard so she can wield her elements. Both of them. The power's just building up inside her with nowhere to go."

"She's *not* using her fire!" With a feral snarl that sounded more like his wolf than the man he was at the moment, Cade started towards the stairs.

Liam followed him, with Caitlin at his heels, and the three argued the entire way to the second floor where their voices faded.

Sinking against the counter, Farren forced a long, slow breath. The next few months were going to be a disaster if she couldn't find Paddy and get some straight answers out of the man.

After another cup of coffee. Because facing Paddy *and* Eli in one day? That was going to take everything she had in her.

CHAPTER FOUR

FARREN

In the years since she'd first met Paddy, she'd never known the man to show his face in town before late afternoon. When he'd rescued her from the woods after Fergus had tried to carve that blasted sigil into her side, it had been well after midnight. He'd tended to her wounds and given her some warm broth, but then he'd disappeared until the sun had started its descent again.

At breakfast, Mara's guilt and shame had cast a pall over the entire group, and Peter, never the most agreeable wolf, had been so restless, at the end of the meal, he'd announced he was heading to Dublin for the week to see a vampire. He'd met the bloke the previous year when Liam had brought the pack to Dublin to hide out.

Farren didn't hold any hope that the vamp would have a feckin' clue how to help them, but one less werewolf in the house for a few days? That would be a blessed relief.

Parking her motorcycle on Doolin's main street, Farren

pulled off her helmet and shook out her hair. The mists covered the beach, but she could hear the waves lap against the shore.

She loved this town. This tiny spot of paradise on Ireland's western coast with its kind people, quiet streets, and lush, green landscapes. But since Fergus had returned and defeating him had drawn the attention of the Thirteen, it hadn't been the same.

Even though she had no elemental powers, she bore the remnants of their mark, and a part of her feared they'd somehow be able to sense her. Or use the scar she'd have for the rest of her life to control her. When they'd found Colin's body, it had born a similar—though more complete—mark, and Fergus had all but admitted the Thirteen had compelled Colin to lure Brian away from the house.

It burned from time to time. Like now. Rubbing her side, she tried to will away the ache, but that only made it worse. She should have been faster. Stronger. Maybe then, Colin would still be alive. Maybe she'd still feel like an alpha.

Her anger intensified with every step towards Doolin House, and by the time she pushed through the establishment's front door, she was about as pissed off as she'd ever been.

Focus. If ya' scare the poor human away, ya' won't find out if the old woman he met was Diedre.

This time of day, the little pub attached to the place was almost empty. Except for a very hung over Eli Escobar. One elbow rested on the table, and he cradled his head in his hand as he stared into a mug of coffee and a plate of eggs and blood sausage.

Poor bastard.

She wasn't sure where that burst of pity came from. After all, he'd run from her office, purposely consumed enough whiskey to end up shattered, and now probably regretted every single one of his life choices.

Don't screw this up.

Farren pulled out a chair across from him and sat down. He groaned, blinked hard to focus on her, and then his eyes widened. "Fuck me. I knew I should have left last night."

"Last night, ya' were drunk off yer arse." Farren snatched the mug of coffee away from him and took a healthy sip. "Today, ya' don't look much better."

"Give that here." Eli held out his hand, his fingers shaking slightly. "Are all werewolves this cruel?"

Farren cringed and glanced around the small space. "Keep yer voice down. Only half of Doolin knows about werewolves."

"Oh. Only *half?*" Eli shoved his plate away and reached for the coffee again. This time, Farren relented. "I don't want any trouble. As soon as I'm not...impaired, I'm heading back to London."

"Don't."

"Don't what?" The man's green eyes—bloodshot now—narrowed. "Ms. Denair, I'm not sure what you're playing at, but I didn't come here to be attacked by a mythical creature I don't even truly believe exists. If you were trying to scare me away, good on you. But now it seems like you want me to stick around, and I can't understand why."

Farren snorted. "*Want* ya' to stick around? No. But ya' have information I need, Escobar, and I don't give up easily. As for the 'mythical creature' shite, finish up those eggs and meet me back at my office. I'll prove to ya' werewolves are very much real."

Shoving back from the table, she turned on a heel and marched out of Doolin House, hoping she'd given him just enough to be curious about.

When she cast a brief glance back over her shoulder, her lips curved into a smile. Eli was handing his credit card to the server while staring back at her.

Just wait, ya' pompous arse. I'll have ya' eatin' those words of yers soon enough.

ELI

He couldn't get out of the pub fast enough. Not that he knew why he was rushing. The PI's office was all of two blocks away, and he could still see her—and the way her shapely arse moved in tight leather pants. She was a study in opposites. Confident, yet when she'd admitted she needed information from him, a hint of vulnerability had seeped into her tone. Even more interesting, it had appeared to piss her off.

The silver wolf—her shoulder-length hair at least matched the nickname—slammed her office door with him only four steps away.

"Listen, Ms. Denair," he said, his voice rough as he yanked on the heavy brass handle, prepared to let her know exactly what he thought of her attitude. Until his brain caught up with his eyes and he realized she was standing in the center of her office, naked as the day she was born. Her clothes lay in a pile next to her, boots tossed haphazardly in front of her desk.

"You wanted proof? Close the feckin' door."

"I...you're..." His cheeks flamed red hot and once he'd done as she'd ordered, he wasn't sure if he should turn back around.

"Ya' can watch. If ye're brave enough. And ya' should know...if ya' try to run, my wolf can open that door. She *will* catch ya'."

Swallowing hard, he spun around, certain he was about to regret every single thing he'd done since rescuing that surfer.

Eli kept his gaze locked on Farren's eyes. Or tried to. But fuck. She was beautiful. Creamy skin, long legs, the right amount of curves.

And then she dropped to her hands and knees and let out a groan. Her skin started to ripple. Like something inside her was desperate to escape.

His mouth went dry, and he stopped breathing when the distinct sound of breaking bones started. Thoughts short-circuited even as they pinged around in his head like lasers bouncing off mirrors.

All that gorgeous silvery white hair disappeared, and her face changed. Her nose lengthened, the tip turning black. Her delicate fingers popped and cracked and changed into paws.

Fur sprouted all over her body, and shite on a stick. She had a tail.

His legs gave out, and he hit the ground with an audible *oof*, still unable to look away as a massive, proud, and fucking magnificent animal sat up panting.

If he'd been able to move, he'd have run, despite her warning, but his body refused to listen to his brain, so he sat stock still when the animal padded over to him.

She—for once he looked into her gray eyes, there was no doubt in his mind this wolf *was* Farren Denair—nosed his shoulder and made a questioning sound. Not exactly a bark or a growl, but there was a hint of a threat in the tone.

"I believe you." He had to force the words out, and the urge to touch her, to stroke her fur, was almost overwhelming.

Farren sat and nodded, then yipped softly and nudged his hand.

"It's all right if I...?"

Another nod.

"Fuck me." The wolf was soft. Softer than he thought the woman could ever be. She almost preened when he ran his fingers over the top of her head, but as he reached her side and felt the raised contours of what he thought might be scars, she growled low in her throat, backed away quickly, and dropped down to her belly.

The shift was as horrifying and mesmerizing as before, but at least this time, he forced himself to avert his eyes once she lay naked on the carpet.

"I'm decent," she said a few moments later, and held out her hand in front of his face.

Eli wasn't proud that he needed her help to stand, but he took it, and as they touched, he felt a strong urge to hold on. Or pull her closer. But he was also convinced she could kill him without batting an eye, so he took a seat in her visitor's chair while she fiddled with a coffee pot in the corner of the office.

The rich scent of the brew steadied him, and when she set a cup in front of him, he risked meeting her gaze. "I should apologize, I suppose."

"That would be a good start."

"Are there any other...'mythical creatures' I should know about?" He didn't want an answer. Not truly. But he had to ask.

Farren sank into her leather chair and started ticking her fingers one by one. "Vampires, elementals, practitioners—commonly called witches by humans—fae, sprites, ghosts..." she pursed her lips briefly before adding, "yetis."

"Yetis?" Coffee threatened to exit his nose at great speed, but he choked on the sip just in time. "What about the Loch Ness Monster?"

"Nessie? She's an elephant who got stuck in Scotland years ago and decided she loved to swim. Nothin' mythical about her."

"Oh. Well, that's reassuring."

You sound like a complete dolt. Snap out of it.

Despite his inner voice yelling at him, he couldn't seem to form any coherent or intelligent questions, and after a full minute of awkward silence, Farren sighed. "Is it all right if I call ya' Eli?"

"Fine. And...?"

"Farren. No one calls me Ms. Denair." After another sip of coffee, she reached into her pocket, withdrew a folded piece of paper, and spread it out in front of him. "Is this the old woman ya' saw in the Greenwich pub?"

The drawing was a bit rough—not unlike his memories—but the likeness was uncanny. "It is."

"Then you, Eli, have some purpose here, and if we don't find out what it is, a number of people I care about could pay the price."

FARREN

Eli's bronzed skin paled, but to his credit, he sat up a little straighter. "What do you mean 'pay the price'?"

She wasn't sure how much to tell him. Somewhere between nothing and everything?

"A few months ago, an earth elemental by the name of Fergus Tharp came to town, and within a week, he'd killed three. Includin' my beta, Colin." Saying the words made her heart hurt, but she held Eli's gaze, refusing to give in to the almost overwhelming wave of grief.

"Your...beta?" Confusion pinched his brows. "I don't understand."

"Ya' know nothin' about wolves? About packs?"

"Am I supposed to? I have a degree from Cambridge, Farren. In art history. The animal kingdom wasn't covered in any of my classes."

"Ya' don't have to be condescending." Restless, she got to her feet and started to pace the length of her office as Eli swiveled his chair around. "Most werewolves are a part of a pack. Within the pack, we've an alpha and a beta. I take it ya' can figure out who's in charge out of the two?"

"Now who's being condescending?"
Point: Eli.

"I'm the alpha of the Doolin pack." She stood up a little straighter on instinct, even though she wasn't sure she could call herself an alpha anymore with half her pack gone. "Colin, he was one of my oldest friends, and the best damn beta. And Fergus Tharp killed him. Right after he tried to do the same to me."

Eli leaned forward, and concern darkened his emerald eyes. "Is that where you got that scar?"

Her hand went instinctively to her side, and pain snaked all around her torso. "Saw that, did ya'? I thought ya' were bein' a gentleman."

That brought a spot of color back to his cheeks. "I tried."

With a strained chuckle, she let him off the hook. "Ya' had permission. Better ya' understood quickly than fight with me all day."

"So, that's a yes?" he asked.

"Ya' know it is." Farren wasn't sure how much more of his shite she could take before bringing him right to Caitlin and letting her work her air charms on the man.

"I'm sorry you lost your...beta. But what does that have to do with me and the old woman at the pub?" There was genuine regret in his tone, and for a moment, she softened her attitude.

Until she squeezed her eyes shut and saw Fergus's face as he carved a part of the sigil into her side. The glee. The sick, disgusting smile and his sing-song voice. Fuck. She'd never forget that voice. It haunted her dreams.

"That woman was a practitioner. And we've been lookin' for her ever since Fergus met his end. If we don't find her, a group of practitioners callin' themselves the Thirteen might come searchin' for...people I care about, and we won't be able to defend ourselves."

"You just threatened to chase me down and tear me apart," he said sharply. "And you're telling me you can't defend yourself? Hardly."

"Against practitioners?" Farren scoffed, and the urge to grab the bottle of whiskey in her bottom desk drawer and top off her coffee welled up stronger than she wanted to admit. "Ya' don't mess with practitioners, Eli. No one does. This scar?" She yanked the hem of her sweater up far enough she could see the edges of the sigil, and swallowed the panic rising inside her. "If Fergus had finished the damned thing, the Thirteen would have been able to control everythin' I did. They could have forced me to murder my family, to hunt down elementals to be tortured and killed…"

The rest of what she wanted to say caught in her throat, and Eli stood, blocking her path. When he reached for her hand, she hissed, "Don't touch me."

"Farren. Take a deep breath."

She couldn't. Not if her life depended on it. With a shake of her head, she sidestepped him, but he matched her movements.

"I won't hurt you." He offered her his hand once more, and this time, she couldn't ignore the honest concern in his voice. Taking a risk, she let him link their fingers and draw her over to the well-worn leather sofa opposite the coffee machine. "Sit. I'll get you a refill."

The caffeine wouldn't help much, but the familiarity, the taste…it often settled her, and she sank back against the cushions while he retrieved her mug and topped it off. When he returned, he sat close enough she could feel the heat of him seep into her. And the man's scent. What was it? Spicy. Woodsy. It brought memories of her first run through the woods behind her property. Freedom and wild abandon.

Back then, she'd been at peace. She'd known who she was. Had a purpose. An ache welled up deep inside her as Eli sat quietly, not touching her, not trying to get her to talk about her feelings.

After a couple of sips of coffee, she forced a long, slow breath. "The past few months have gone sideways, and havin' to explain things…"

"I wish I could say you didn't have to go on, but I have no

bloody clue what an elemental is. Or how I'm supposed to help you find this practitioner. *She* found *me* in that pub, and she disappeared before I could ask her to explain why I had to come here."

Eli dug in his pocket and pulled out a small velvet pouch. "She gave me this. And told me the silver wolf would need it."

Once he loosened the ties, he upended the bag over Farren's outstretched palm. The silver pendant drew a sharp gasp from her lips, and her gaze darted from the intricately crafted tree of life to Eli and back again. She'd seen this image before.

Stamped in the corner of half a dozen pages of Diedre's book.

CHAPTER FIVE

*B*ringing Eli back to her house was a bad idea. Cade and Liam would be pissed, but the silver pendant in her hand was proof the man next to her had a purpose here.

"Can ya' stay in town for a few days?" she asked, running her thumb over the glittering charm.

"I work for myself. My agent will expect to hear from me, but he doesn't need me back in London for at least another month." Flexing his fingers on his thighs, he continued. "I need to work. I'm not someone who can sit idle. But along with sculpting, I create sand art, and you have a lovely beach across from the hotel."

"Sand art?" She couldn't help herself. The very idea of playing in the sand as a job was so foreign to her.

He pulled out his phone and brought up a photo of a massive phoenix under gray skies. "This was the last piece I created before everything went pear-shaped."

The majestic creature looked alive. She could imagine it breathing, dripping flames as it flew over the countryside. Trying *not* to show how very impressed she was, she nodded. "Nice."

"I'm so glad it meets your approval." With a noise that was half snort and half huff, he shoved the phone back into his pocket. "That was a solid eight hours of physical labor, for your information."

Be nice. You need him.

With a sigh, she stared down at her own hands clasped in her lap. "Small talk isn't one of my talents."

"Clearly." After a beat, he shook his head. "Apologies, Farren. I'm shattered. If I'm staying, I should make sure Doolin House has a room for me for the week. And perhaps take a kip."

Farren studied him. "Ye're an odd mix, Eli. Some of yer words are so very British, but I swear ya' have a hint of the Irish in ya'."

His eyes clouded over and he ran a hand over his dark locks. "I spent my formative years in boarding school just outside of London. But from what my barrister has told me, my mum was Irish and my father was Puerto Rican."

"From what your barrister told you?"

His frown carried pain, along with uncertainty. "I don't remember my parents. Or anything before my fourteenth year. They were killed in a car accident. I was in a coma for a week, and when I came out of it, my life was a complete mystery to me. Still is, if I'm honest."

Mysteries were both fascinating and potentially dangerous. Given how much peril she'd experienced in the past few months, adding more seemed...unwise.

Farren rose and went to her desk, then scribbled her address on a scrap of paper. "Show up here after 5:00 p.m. *Not* before. Ya' understand? There are four other werewolves livin' with me, and they don't take to strangers. If ya' get there before me, I can't guarantee they won't bite yer head clean off."

For good measure, she added her mobile to the note. "And if ya' oversleep, ya' call me."

"Right." Eli swallowed hard, his cheeks paling once more. "Not before 5:00 p.m."

"And if ya' try to skip town, I'll hunt ya' down. Me *and* my wolf."

She should be kinder to the man, but the alpha in her needed to assert her dominance. Besides, a healthy dose of fear would help keep the man from dying when he met Cade and Liam. At least she hoped it would.

Getting blood out of her hardwood floors would *not* be easy and she didn't need the extra hassle. At least that's what she told herself. She wasn't...*concerned* about his safety. Or acknowledging the softness she felt deep down when she looked at him. No. Not at all.

"Don't be late," she said as she held her office door open for him.

"I'm never late."

Coming from any other man, Farren would have laughed at the words. But Eli? The conviction in his tone impressed her. As did the intensity of his stare. He was close enough for his scent to wrap itself around her, and instinct took over.

Reaching for his hand, she tugged him closer, and he crushed his lips to hers. Eli's strong arm caught her around the waist and held her against him. A groan rumbled in his throat, and she parted her lips and let him in, taking as much as she gave.

Her arm draped around his neck, and she was seconds from wrapping her legs around his waist when she came to her senses and pushed away from him.

His chest heaved, straining the dark gray Henley to its limits.

"I'm sorry," he managed, his voice hoarse. "I didn't mean to take liberties."

"I think I took as many myself." Shaking her head and clenching her hands into fists, she reined in her raging emotions. "No more of that. I expect ya' at five. And...we're not talkin' about what just happened. Ever. Nor is it happenin' again."

"No. Definitely not." With one last strained smile, he gave her a small bow and then darted out the door.

"Well, fuck. Feckin' inconvenient, that." Snagging her bag from her desk drawer, she headed for O'Connor's Pub. She needed a drink. Badly.

O'CONNOR'S WASN'T busy this time of day. The lunch rush wouldn't start for another hour, and Farren took her customary seat in the corner of the back room.

"What'll it be, Farren?" Mickey, the owner, asked. "Or is this one of those 'Leave me the fuck alone' days?"

"A pint of the black with a whiskey chaser. And a plate of chips." She glanced around the mostly empty space. "Don't suppose you've seen Paddy around?"

"Not for weeks. The band's been missin' him. That arse never keeps to a schedule." Mickey shook his head as he walked away. "If ya' find him before I do, tell him he owes me twenty euro."

"Put it on my tab," she called after him. For everything Paddy had done for her, she could cover his bar bill. A part of her hoped he'd sense the imbalance and come to rectify it. Stranger things had happened with the man. Hell, Farren didn't even know *what* he was. Practitioner? Fae? Both?

The chips helped settle her stomach as she used her phone to search for information on different meanings for the tree of life when intermingled with the Irish trinity knot. But before long, she gave up. There were simply too many different interpretations. Maybe Caitlin would have more luck.

She sent the air elemental a photo of the pendant along with a message. *"Diedre gave this to Eli. It's got to mean something. Be home in an hour or so unless I find Paddy."*

Caitlin responded in under two minutes. *"Are you bringing Eli with you?"*

"No. But he'll be around at five. Wanted time to warn Cade and Liam. And convince them not to murder the poor man."

"Solid plan. I'll talk to Liam. You might want to be back here by 3:00. Cade's going to call the rest of the pack."

Great. Farren rolled her eyes. She didn't want to get mixed up in Cade's pack politics. He'd ordered two of his wolves to stay in Seattle, and two more—along with their pup—to head for Canada. From the little she'd gathered from Caitlin, they were all pissed about it. Unsurprising.

"The silver one seeks answers."

Farren jerked, her fingers knocking half a dozen chips onto the table. She'd been so mired in her thoughts, she hadn't heard the pub door open. Then again, perhaps it hadn't.

"Paddy, ya' daft bastard. Ya' scared the piss outta me."

"Old Paddy meant no harm." The elderly man pulled out a chair, sat, and withdrew his spoons from the inside pocket of his tweed jacket. "The time is close now."

"What time?" Fuck. What she wouldn't give for one straight, honest, direct conversation with him. Every time, he spoke in riddles and vague references that only made sense hours or days later.

"The time for secrets is almost over. What is blind will find a way to see. What is hidden will be the answer to all." He rapped the spoons on his thigh and smiled a mostly toothless grin.

"Gone for weeks, and ya' still can't give me a straight answer to anythin'? Ya' show up at my front door with Diedre so her magic can protect Mara and Caitlin, then vanish without even sayin' goodbye. We can't read that feckin' book ya' know. The pages keep changin'.'"

"Need a key, ya' do. And the sight that only comes with trustin' yer heart."

"Any idea where this key is?" Farren tossed back the whiskey, then signaled to Mickey for another two shots. One for her and one for Paddy. The man tended to keep talking whenever the drinks were flowing.

"Old Paddy knows, but cannot say."

Slamming her glass down on the table, she leaned closer and hissed, "Then what good are ya'? For years, I've trusted ya'. Let ya' go on with yer riddles and mysteries, but enough now. Liam almost died. Mara's gone away in the head, and now Diedre sends a man to town with this feckin' thing," she held up the pendant, letting it swing from her fingers and catch the light, "but doesn't tell him why."

Paddy moved so quickly, Farren didn't have time to react, snatching the bauble from her hand and closing his fingers around it. His cloudy eyes cleared, and he focused on her with such intensity, she stifled her retort. "A pretty thing, but not for show. Only whole will power grow. He's the last, and doesn't know. Teach him or give in to woe."

"Another goddamn mystery."

When he offered her the pendant, she returned it to the velvet pouch in her pocket. The old man pushed to his feet, and Farren reached for his hand. "Come back to the house with me, Paddy. Please. We need yer help."

He smiled even as he shook his head. "Paddy's got the wrong time. But he'll see ya' again."

Farren's fingers fell away, despite her efforts to hold on to the man, and once again, she wondered what powers he could muster. Clearly he'd whispered to her mind somehow, but she hadn't sensed an air charm, or smelled the metallic scent of magic.

Magic it had to be, though, because he shuffled out of the bar and she remained glued to her seat.

"Feckin' loon. One day, I'm goin' to figure him out." She just hoped it wasn't too late when she did.

CHAPTER SIX

*S*itting at the counter peeling apples—enough for at least three pies—she felt almost *normal*. Except for Cade refusing to go more than twenty feet from her and Caitlin checking on her every half an hour.

She understood their concern. Hell, she hated this as much or more than they did. Never knowing when she'd lose herself? When she'd be forced into a dark, terrifying place where she could see everything around her, but had no control over what her sister's fire element wanted her to do?

Farren strode through the front door, her silvery blond hair cascading behind her as she pulled off her motorcycle helmet. "Well, I found the bastard. And then he disappeared right in front of me. Again."

"Paddy?" Liam asked.

"Who else do ya' think? Daft old man spouted some nonsense about how we needed a key to read the book, but wouldn't tell me what it was or where to find it. And more malarkey about the blind bein' able to see. Oh, and this. I wrote this part down." She unfolded a piece of paper she'd tucked into her pocket. "A pretty thing, but not for show. Only whole will power grow. He's the last, and doesn't know. Teach him or give in to woe."

"What the fuck is that supposed to mean?" Cade came up behind Mara and draped his arm around her shoulders. "You okay, honey?" he whispered in her ear.

"I'm fine. But this is nice." She snuggled against his chest, letting the touch of her mate, his warmth, his strength, center her. Besides Caitlin's charms, Cade's presence was the only thing that worked. Except when it didn't. Like this morning. When she'd wriggled out from under his arm, left their bed, and walked outside, barefoot, not dressed for the chill, and with no clear idea of where she was going.

All the while screaming inside her own head for whatever invisible force had locked her away to release her. To stay safely within the boundaries of Diedre's wards.

A tiny impact somewhere just below her navel made her laugh. "She's kicking again." Guiding Cade's hand to her stomach, she only had to wait a few seconds for the baby to recognize his presence and push against his palm.

"That will never not be amazing." Cade nuzzled her neck and bit down lightly, sending need arcing through her. "I love you, honey. Always and no matter what."

Tears stung her eyes. *No matter what. Like what if I wander so far, the Thirteen can find me? What if they take the baby? What if I get hit by a car and lose her that way? What if—*

The second bite was harder, and he held on until she took a deep breath. "Stop worrying. We'll figure this out. I promise."

"You can't promise." She turned in his arms, the apples forgotten, and rested her forehead against his. "If whatever's taking control of me gets strong enough, it could hurt you. Kill you."

"Won't happen. I'm tougher than I look."

Her laugh escaped despite her fears. "You look pretty tough, shaggy man. All those muscles."

Cade stood up a little straighter, prouder, and the raw desire, the desperate need to possess her and claim her again and again churned in his ice blue eyes. "All those muscles aren't half as strong as my love, Mara. You have to know that."

"I do."

If only she knew *anything* else.

"It's almost time," Liam said as he set up his laptop on the table and Caitlin brought chairs around for everyone. "Livie should be callin' any moment."

From where she was sitting, she could see the screen, so she continued peeling and chopping the apples while Cade took a seat next to Liam. As if by tacit agreement—or maybe they had worked all of this out ahead of time—Tierney ambled into the kitchen and leaned against the counter across from her, and Ewan braced himself along the wall by the back door.

Just in case I wander off.

She hated that they were so concerned, but had to admit they were simply being careful. And no matter how much it stung not to be trusted to be alone for even a few minutes outside of the bathroom, she knew she needed their protection. More and more each day.

THE VIDEO CALL CONNECTED, **and Livie and Shawn's faces filled** one half of the screen with the top of Serena's head bobbing in and out of focus. Her blond hair had started to curl, and Mara's eyes stung, yet again. She'd already missed almost two months of the baby's life, and she covered her mouth with her hand and blinked back tears. Damn emotions. Pregnancy made them so much worse. She wasn't a crier. Or...hadn't been. Now, it was all she did. That and make Cade worry.

The other half of the screen blinked to life, and Christine and Ollie sat at the pack's kitchen table. Ollie's lips moved, but no sound came from the computer, and Cade and Livie said in tandem, "Ollie, you're muted."

The older werewolf's cheeks flushed bright red, and he tapped his screen. "I hate this stupid computer."

Shawn said something Mara couldn't hear, and Livie elbowed him in the side. "Shut it. Like you're much better with the TV remote."

God, Mara had missed this. The banter. Family. Peter mostly kept to himself, and though she'd become close with Caitlin, the poor air elemental spent most of her time either trying to translate Diedre's book or working her charms to keep Mara stable. Though Mara and Liam had forgiven one another for the rocky introduction they'd had, she wasn't sure they'd ever be quite comfortable around each other.

"Livie," Mara said, sliding off the stool. "Hold Serena a little higher? I need to see those cheeks."

The blond werewolf grinned and helped Serena balance on chubby little legs. "She's finally sleeping through the night. And she got her first tooth!" Shawn leaned closer and skimmed his finger along Serena's chin to make the baby laugh. The tooth peeked out for just a second, and Mara's heart melted.

She rested her hand on Cade's shoulder, and he reached back to squeeze her fingers. "Kiss her for me, Liv."

"Wait. I need to see the bump!" Livie called out when Mara tried to withdraw silently and return to the apples. Of all the members of the pack, Livie had taken to Mara the fastest, and the two had bonded over Livie's pregnancy. It didn't hurt that Serena never cried in Mara's arms. The pup already recognized Cade as the pack's alpha, and with his scent all over Mara, she always behaved when Mara watched her.

As Livie squealed and gushed over how great Mara looked, how she couldn't wait until the two pups could play together, Mara realized what she'd been missing since they'd left Seattle. Since the elementals in Oregon had tried to drug her and take her from Cade, since they'd fled to Ireland. Her friends. Livie, Jen, Adam and his wife, Lisa. Her Aunt Lillian.

But it was more than that. She ached to be...*normal* again. As normal as she could be, at least with two elements inside of her and mated to a werewolf.

"I wish I could be there," Livie said as she touched her screen. "I miss you."

"Miss you too." Mara could barely get the words out over the lump in her throat. God, she wanted a hug. Girl talk. To curl up on the couch and talk about nothing important. And everything. All at the same time.

The next few minutes were pure chaos, everyone talking at once, just like pack meals had been back home. It was too much. Too hard to know she might never be with them all again. Mara returned to the apples, determined not to let this deep, abiding sadness win. For Cade's sake, at least.

"Bossman?" Livie asked when the conversation started to wane. "When can we all go home?"

Rubbing the back of his neck, Cade looked to Liam, then to Mara. She hated seeing such pain in his eyes. All because she couldn't control the fire inside her.

"We don't know. Caitlin and Tierney are still trying to read Diedre's book, but until we know the Thirteen isn't going to come after Mara...this is the only place we're safe."

"Shawn and I could come—"

"No," Cade growled. "It's too dangerous for you to bring the pup here. You're safe in Canada. At least as far as we know."

Shawn cleared his throat. "The pack up in Anchorage has met an elemental or two over the years, and they've agreed to make some calls, see if anyone's heard of the Thirteen."

"Good. Christine, how'd you manage with the sigils Caitlin taught you?"

"Fine," the werewolf healer said. "And that strange smell hasn't been back."

Weeks ago, Ollie and Christine, who were still living at the pack house, had come home to a heavy metallic odor hanging in the air of every room. Practitioner magic. Locator spells to sense Mara, Caitlin had thought.

"Good." Cade relaxed slightly, and Mara let herself turn her focus to the pies. It was easier than listening to her family talking about her like she wasn't even there. Their voices faded into the background, and she started to relax. Until Cade's fingers wrapped around her wrist so tightly, she gasped.

"Mara! Fuck, honey. I called your name four times. You were...*there* again, weren't you? Holding a knife."

The agony etched on his face was too much. But so was his tone. As soon as he'd eased the knife from her hand, she jerked back. "No. *This* was not my sister's fire. *This* was me tuning out because I can't stand it when you all talk *around* me rather than *to* me. It was being exhausted because I'm up every two hours to pee. Because at 5:30 this morning, I got shoved into a prison I couldn't escape and had to watch myself wander the house for an hour, then walk right down the driveway, barefoot. Because Caitlin had to charm me to get me to rest. Because I slept through breakfast and had the worst morning sickness in a month when I finally woke up.

"*This* was missing my home. Our bed. My favorite sweater. The fuzzy blanket on the back of our couch. Hell, *this* was me missing my best fucking friend. Aunt Lil. Livie, Chrissy, Serena. *This* was hating that I can't even muster joy for our baby! She doesn't deserve this. None of us do."

She held up her hands when Cade reached for her. The last thing she wanted at the moment was him comforting her. She needed the anger. It made her feel...normal.

"Honey, you have to calm down."

"I do *not*. You're not my alpha, remember? You're my mate. My husband. You're supposed to support me, not smother me in bubble wrap because you're afraid I'm going to break."

Cade growled, and Caitlin darted between the two of them. "Wait. Mara's right."

"What?" Mara stared at the air elemental in disbelief. She loved Caitlin. The two had developed a mostly easy friendship complicated only by the frequency with which Caitlin had to work her charms on Mara.

With a weak smile, Caitlin met Mara's gaze. "When we met...when I was first Caitlin again, you fought for me. You fought the rest of the pack for my right to be heard. I thought you were so brave and I was the complete opposite." She turned to Cade. "Since we...ended Fergus, Mara's been different. Not herself. *This?* This is your mate fighting to survive, Cade. I know I don't have any right to say this, but you need to let her."

Anger and frustration flashed in Cade's eyes for a beat, along with the silver and gold flecks of his wolf. His knuckles cracked, and Mara feared he was about to shift. Until it was like a switch flipped, and the tension melted from his shoulders.

"Fuck. I'm sorry, honey. I didn't realize... I have to protect you. It's who I am. I thought if I were strong enough, I could keep you safe, but I'm not, and it's killing me."

"You're the strongest man I know," Mara murmured. "But you can't fight this battle for me. You can be there with me, but you can't take my place."

Cade nodded, and though Mara would bet her life they'd fight about this again, for now, he seemed to understand.

Livie cleared her throat. "Mara? Why don't we FaceTime. I'll grab my phone. Shawn can fill me in on any pack business later. And Cade can do the same for you."

Turning towards the screen, Mara offered Livie a grateful

smile. "I'd really like that. Give me just a minute to get up to our room."

"Mara—" Cade's voice carried a heavy warning, but Livie stopped him.

"Shawn's staying on the call, bossman. If Mara looks like she's disappearing on me, all I have to do is call for him and he'll tell you. She needs this. And so do I."

Mara's phone rang, and as soon as the call connected, Serena's chubby face filled the screen. The baby flailed her arms and babbled happily, and Mara swiped away a tear. "Hi, sweetie."

Before she could take more than two steps towards the stairs, Cade was at her back, his arm wrapped around her waist, palm on her belly. Their pup kicked inside her, and he whispered in her ear. "I love you, honey. You're strong, and I'm sorry I forgot that."

With one last gentle scrape of his teeth to her neck, he released her, and Mara headed for their room as Livie's face came into better focus. "We're not going more than a couple of days without talking from now on. I've missed you, Mara. So has Serena. And I don't just mean your babysitting."

It felt so good to laugh, and she found a small bit of hope in Livie's smile. Maybe it would all be okay. Maybe she could find a way to hold on to herself. Maybe she wouldn't lose everything.

CHAPTER SEVEN

ELI

$\mathcal{H}$e really should have slept. But every time he tried, he found himself thinking about Farren and that kiss. He wasn't one to sleep around—or kiss women he'd only just met. Though he'd taken several lovers—including a man or two—at university and in the years beyond, the only time he'd ever been this impulsive was a few months before he'd received his degree.

Percy had been a year behind him, but the man had a brilliant eye for art, and they'd met at a traveling Van Gogh exhibit. The attraction had started like a wildfire, but the next morning, they'd gone their separate ways.

Standing on the sidewalk three meters above the beach, he wondered why they hadn't exchanged numbers and found he couldn't remember much of their final conversation.

A side effect of the accident that stole his parents from him? Hell, he wished he had even a single memory of them. Of the time before he woke in the hospital.

Because at the moment, he felt untethered and alone, and though he had a few friends back in London, he wasn't particularly close to anyone. Getting to know someone was hard when any talk about childhoods and the past was only one sided.

He still had a little over an hour before he was due at Farren's, and his GPS informed him the drive would be less than ten minutes. The weather had turned bright and almost warm, and he took the stairs down to the sand, stripped out of his shoes and socks, and stood barefoot at the edge of the sea.

This stretch of beach was largely protected by a curved berm of land, and the waves died a good fifty meters out, gently lapping at his feet. He dug his toes deeper into the sand, and some of his exhaustion faded. The ocean breezes always refreshed him.

Water started to wick its way up his khakis, and he stepped back, scanning the long strip of beach. There. A piece of driftwood almost as thick as his forearm rested against a gathering of rocks like it was waiting for him.

He had no idea if the Garda would stop him, but he had to create. Had to touch something *real*.

Lines and curves formed from his efforts. His shoulders ached, his biceps burned, and his mind wandered. He never planned his creations, preferring to rely on his instincts rather than sophisticated CAD programs or even concept drawings.

The driftwood cracked into two pieces, and Eli stepped back to survey his creation.

"Fuck me."

The wolf stood tall and proud, her paws close to the water and her head only a meter from the rocks. The sand didn't do her unique silver fur justice, but he'd captured the nap of it, how soft it had felt under his fingers.

Dropping to his knees, he stroked his hand along the top of her head. The ground under him felt like it was rippling, and the longer he knelt there, the stronger the vibrations became.

In minutes, the wolf faded into oblivion, the beach returning to its natural state, and Eli started to shiver. Panic twisted in his stomach. This was the third earthquake he'd experienced in ten days, and he'd felt each down to his soul.

Pushing to his feet, he staggered back against the rocks, wiped his brow, and checked the time. Bollocks. He needed a shower before going to see Farren. And a cup of the strongest tea Doolin House could brew.

FARREN

After the strangest pack meeting she'd ever encountered—video chat wouldn't be her choice, even with her wolves scattered to the winds—Caitlin and Tierney lingered. "Well, let's see it, then," Caitlin said.

Farren dug in her pocket for the velvet pouch, and when she held it in her hand, she could feel the power thrumming through her. "Paddy gave me one of his feckin' riddles when he saw this. 'A pretty thing, but not for show. Only whole will power grow. He's the last, and doesn't know. Teach him or give in to woe.'"

"And him would be…this Eli bloke?" Tierney asked.

"Hell if I know. But he'll be here in a few minutes. Ya' warned Liam, yeah?" The last thing she needed was the two men beating Eli to a bloody pulp.

"He growled a bit. So did Cade." Caitlin huffed. "Ya' would think hearin' Diedre sent him would be enough. But apparently not."

Farren's eye roll was almost painful. "They're both newly mated. That's the only excuse I'll give either of them."

Taking the pendant, Caitlin led them into Farren's study

where she and Tierney had papers spread out over the large antique desk and taped to all four walls.

"Ya've turned my office into a feckin' research library?" She'd been avoiding this room for weeks now, not willing to be reminded of her failures as an alpha. As a werewolf. If she'd been faster when Fergus had attacked them all at Diedre's, Liam might never have been taken and tortured for more than a day. He might not walk with a permanent limp or have nightmares he hadn't admitted to anyone. Farren had heard him a time or two.

"We woulda' used the kitchen, but cookin' with all this paper around? We'd make a bloody mess of the place," Tierney said with a shrug of his shoulders. "And ya' never come in here."

Farren schooled her features so her devoted young wolf wouldn't see how much his words stung. He was a good kid. No. A good man.

"No need with another alpha in the house," she muttered.

Caitlin opened the book to the first page with the tree of life symbol and placed the pendant next to the drawing. Nothing happened. The page looked exactly the same.

"Well, Paddy was right about this bein' pretty," Caitlin said. "But if it's 'not for show' shouldn't it be doin' somethin'?"

The doorbell rang before Farren could suggest they try another page, and she took off at a run. If Cade or Liam got there first, they'd scare the piss out of Eli. Or worse. Growl at him and threaten to tear him apart.

Caitlin and Tierney started to follow, but Farren whirled around steps from the door. "No. Ya' can all wait in the living room. The man didn't know a damn thing about werewolves until this mornin'. I'm not lettin' him be ambushed when he might be able to help us."

Tierney immediately stared down at the hardwood floor. "Ye're right. I'll get everyone together."

Before Caitlin followed him, she inhaled deeply and stirred

the air with a light twist of her fingers. "There's something... familiar about him. His scent. But I don't know what it is. Ya' made sure he wasn't a practitioner, yeah?"

"I'm not that daft," Farren snapped. "And Paddy said we were to teach him. Go wait with the others."

Farren's wolf was ready for a fight. Caitlin must have seen the change in Farren's eyes, because she held up her hands and backed away. "I'm sorry. I had to ask."

Caitlin might not be a part of her pack, but by rights, Farren could assert her dominance over everyone in her house except for Cade. The two were equals in strength and bloodline.

Not pausing to acknowledge the apology, Farren covered the last few steps to the door and pulled it open.

Eli stood on the flagstones with his hands in his pockets. In the few hours since she'd last seen him, he must not have had his "kip," because he looked like he was about to fall over.

"Are ya' all right?" she asked as she gestured for the man to come in.

"Been a rough afternoon." He didn't elaborate, and she didn't push. Not yet, anyway. Cade and Liam wouldn't be patient for long. "But I'm here. Ready to be thrown to the wolves. Quite literally, it seems."

"Oh, stop worryin'. I won't let them hurt ya'. They *will* growl and snap a bit." She forced a smile, but Eli wasn't amused if the sound of his teeth grinding together was any indication.

Leading him down the hall, she tried to ignore her pounding heart. This man held some significance in their fight, but there was more to her nervousness than simply wanting to protect Caitlin and Mara from the Thirteen. She just wished she knew why she couldn't get the man out of her head.

Cade and Liam stood behind their mates who were seated next to one another on one of the leather sofas on either side of the hearth. "Everyone, this is Eli," Farren said when the two of them were standing in front of the fireplace. "Cade and his mate, Mara. Liam and his Caitlin. And the two wolves in my pack, Tierney and Ewan. Cade and Liam have their own pack based in Seattle, but they're here until we can make sure Mara's safe from the Thirteen."

Eli stared at Farren with such intensity, she almost looked away, but the alpha wolf in her refused to even contemplate showing such weakness. If anything, the animal inside wanted to take control and show Eli exactly who was in charge here.

"From the witches. I don't understand, Farren. All I know of witches is from the *Wizard of Oz*. In my world, they fly on broomsticks and have warts and black cats. How are these witches going to come after Mara. And why?"

"I'm an elemental," Mara said. "Did Farren explain what that means?"

"No." His entire body coiled, tightened, like he was expecting someone to attack him, but Mara only held out a hand and conjured a few drops of water to spin and tumble around over her palm. Next to her, Caitlin flexed her fingers and stirred the air, taking the water from Mara and lifting the drops halfway to the ceiling before they disappeared.

"Shite." Eli took a step back, but that just sent him hitting the stone mantle.

Dammit. Farren hadn't realized how she'd unintentionally trapped him. She stood between Eli and the door, and on the other side, Ewan blocked his escape.

Mara picked up her cup of tea, but the baby must have kicked because the saucer tumbled from her grip and landed on the thick floor rug. Eli retrieved it, and when their fingers brushed, Mara shoved the tea cup at Cade and grabbed Eli's hand, her brows furrowed.

"Oh, my God. You're...Earth."

It took a full three seconds for her words to register around the room before chaos took over.

ELI

The two largest men—Cade and Liam if he remembered correctly—leapt over the couch growling. The woman next to Mara rose and a frigid wind pressed him to the hearth with such force, he wasn't sure he could move.

And Farren? The shock in her eyes mixed with betrayal, but she stepped between him and the other two male werewolves.

"Stop this shite right fuckin' now!" There was no mistaking the command in her tone, and the other two men, younger and definitely *not* in charge of anything darted to her sides.

"Farren, ya' know what happened the last time we went up against an Earth elemental," Liam spat and then glanced back at Caitlin. The connection between the two of them was unmistakable. Mate. That's the word Farren had used.

"Yeah, and Fergus was off his rocker." Turning to Eli, she grabbed his shoulders and held him still, but at least the wind died down. He'd started to shiver. "Have somethin' to tell me, Eli?"

"No! I don't know what the fuck you're talking about. I'm *not* an elemental."

Farren leaned closer and sniffed him. *Sniffed? Fuck me. Maybe I did drown and everything since has been the afterlife?*

That didn't make sense either. Eli wasn't certain if he believed in heaven and hell or any sort of existence beyond this one, but he was pretty damn sure it wouldn't be this...strange.

"He doesn't smell like Earth," she said. "Are ya' quite sure, Mara?"

"Yes." She wobbled to her feet, one hand on her belly, and tried to edge around Cade. "Move it, shaggy man. Elemental or not, I don't think Eli came here to hurt me."

"Don't take another step," Cade growled.

"Um, we had this conversation a few hours ago, remember? Not fragile. Also not about to lose myself. If anything, having Eli here is grounding." She sidestepped him, shouldering Liam out of the way in the process, and then she was in front of Farren. "I have no intention of hurting him."

Eli didn't want Farren going anywhere. Not with the way everyone else was staring at him. Thank God all she did was take one step to the side and release her hold on him.

Mara, quite obviously pregnant, held out her hand. "Go ahead. I won't hurt you, Eli."

"Then what *are* you doing?"

Shooting her mate a look that clearly said "shut it," Mara lifted her other hand as well, and Eli would have hit the ground had he not been pushed up against the hearth. Three new water droplets danced in the air, and in Mara's other palm? A tiny flame.

"I carry two elements inside me. And it's going to drive me insane in the end if we can't find some way to stabilize me." With a puff of smoke, the flame disappeared, and Mara waited. "I want to touch you because if you do have Earth, then I'll feel it."

"I don't. I'm as human as they come." Despite his protests, there was something in Mara's tone that he couldn't ignore. A desperation. As a gentle breeze stirred his hair, his panic started to abate and he held out his hand.

Wait. What's happening?

He hadn't intended to move.

"Caitlin, are ya' charmin' him?" Farren's outrage shocked the confusion from his thoughts, and he shoved both hands back into his pockets.

"You lot are insane," Eli said. "I came here to help. To find answers. I don't deserve to be attacked for something I'm not. You have the pendant. Use it. And leave me the fuck alone."

Shoving his way through the press of werewolves and elementals alike, he ran for the door, Farren calling after him.

She seemed to be the only one who didn't want him gone, and even she was pissed. His heartbeat thundered in his ears and he couldn't think clearly until he was in his rental car, speeding down the driveway.

He had to get as far from Doolin as he could. Tonight.

CHAPTER EIGHT

ELI

*B*last it. From the moment he'd left London, he'd known this trip would end badly. But what else could he have done? His flat wasn't safe. The intruders had fled into the night, and the police had no idea who they were or where they'd gone.

Maybe they'd just wanted to nick his laptop?

And somehow ended up with your birth certificate?

He snorted as he turned onto Doolin's main street. If all they'd wanted were material things, they wouldn't have been lying in wait for him.

Eli lived simply. His flat was in a solidly upper-middle class neighborhood, but he didn't care much for material things. The most expensive thing he owned? His mattress. His leather jacket was likely the second most valuable item. Beyond that, he had a four-year-old computer, a handful of knickknacks he'd collected over the years—none of them worth more than twenty euro—and an old guitar his former headmaster had given him.

69

The instrument *was* valuable. But not so valuable that someone would risk jail time for it. His fingers started to tingle as he itched to pick up the guitar and play a few chords. He was rubbish at stringing them together to make actual music, but the act of trying? It calmed him. Almost as much as sculpting. Or working with the sand.

The Doolin House Pub was overflowing on a Friday night, and Eli didn't feel like dealing with all the people to find himself a pint—or any food—so he returned to the beach and sank down onto the rocks far from the water line.

"You're a fucking coward," he muttered, unsure why he'd run in the first place.

Because they accused you of being an elemental. And hiding it.

Why did he care what they accused him of? He wasn't even sure what an elemental was beyond Mara's ability to conjure fire and water out of nothing. And the way Caitlin had forced him back against the hearth with what? Air?

They'd called him earth. He loved working with his hands. With stone. Sand. Anything that came from the earth. But...that didn't make him an elemental. That made him a sculptor.

Eli flattened his palms against the rocks, letting their cool jagged edges soothe him. If he were home in London, he'd be at his studio this very moment, working until his muscles gave out. Until he had nothing left to give.

Under his hands, he imagined a great silver wolf taking shape.

"Blast it! Stop thinking about her."

Farren was a distraction he didn't need. Didn't want. It was too late to drive back to London tonight, but first thing in the morning he'd leave. Despite wanting a drink like he'd never wanted one before, he wouldn't touch a sip because he couldn't let anything delay his departure.

Rising, he sucked in a sharp breath as his hands seemed to be fused to the rocks. With a shout, he wrenched them away, and pain arced from his palms halfway up his arms. Pieces of stone fell away in an intricate pattern, and Eli staggered back.

He'd done the impossible. He'd created the wolf he couldn't drive from his thoughts. Farren. Almost as majestic in rock as she was in real life.

A tremor shook the sand beneath him, and he steadied himself by stroking the wolf's head. He didn't know why he felt such a connection to Farren. She'd brought him to a house where at least two other wolves wanted to kill him. If not more. But he still wanted to see her again. To explain that he *wasn't* an elemental. Had never been one.

"There he is," a hushed voice said into the darkness all around him. "Secure him now. Before he can fight back."

Eli didn't understand why the voice wanted to secure him, but he *was* bloody certain he didn't want to be secured by anyone. Except maybe Farren.

Whirling around, he found himself face to face with a man and a woman. Both wore long dark cloaks, and the woman's light brown hair stirred in the wind. He couldn't clearly see their faces, only the slight form of the woman on the left and the bulk of the man on the right.

"What do you want?" he asked, taking a step back.

"You, of course. We need an earth elemental now that Tharp and his little bitch failed in their task," the woman said. Her voice held a thick Scottish accent, and a chill ran down Eli's spine.

"I'm not an elemental."

Stall. Someone has to come out of Doolin House soon.

But in his heart, Eli knew… No one would come to save him. He wasn't the kind of man people saved. No, he was the kind of man everyone else forgot about.

"Your powers may be bound, but you are an elemental just the same." This from the man. He whispered a few words in a language Eli couldn't understand, and lightning—red lightning —shot from the man's fingers.

Eli could only watch it as it landed squarely in the center of his chest, and the pain. Oh, fuck. He'd never experienced pain like this before. The power was eating its way through him from the inside out, and his arms and legs wouldn't respond to his commands to run. To fight. To do anything.

When he thought he could take no more, he screamed, and the reddish streaks of what?—magic? energy?—flowed out of his hands, his feet, his eyes, ears, and mouth. The scream didn't sound like him, but the pain in his throat told him it had to be his.

Is this how I'm to die?

The man and woman approached slowly, and the power coursing through his body intensified. Flaming hot and icy cold, winding around his bones. Pressure threatened to crush him, and he couldn't breathe.

Help. Someone help!

They were almost close enough to touch him now, and when they did? Would he die? Or worse?

"He's been with them all!" the woman hissed. "Air, Water, and Fire! Secure him, Monroe! He can tell us where the others are. Help us find them, despite that traitorous bitch's handiwork."

"What do you think I am trying to do? His power is bound, and it's resisting me, Glenna."

Eli strained to listen to them—as much as he could with his body feeling like it was about to turn into a lump of charred ash. In the back of his mind, he *knew* he had to pay attention. That whatever they were saying was important. To him. To Farren. To Mara and Caitlin. But the agony twisting every part of him made it hard to string their words into sentences that made sense.

"Must I do *everything?*" Glenna muttered and raised her

hands. Power glowed between her palms, blue this time, and she started to chant.

No. I can't take any more...

His whole body shook, the sands under his feet shifting until he thought he'd surely topple over any second.

This is it. This is my end.

A rhythmic thudding sound came from behind him, followed by a loud snarl, and then Farren leapt over him in her wolf form. Fangs glistened as she curled her lips back and howled, taking Monroe down to the ground with momentum alone. Glenna turned her power against Farren, sending the blue tendrils of power snaking around the wolf's body.

Farren whimpered in pain, and the magic coiled and collected just below her throat. Eli blinked hard. With Monroe moaning from a meter away, his magic was fading, and Eli thought he'd be able to move in another few seconds.

The spot where the magic gathered glowed brighter until it was almost blinding. Farren growled a warning and reared up on two legs.

Blue flames arced towards Glenna and Monroe, and the man prone on the ground screamed. Glenna countered the magic with more of her own. Sparks danced along the sand, and Eli had a passing thought that they might be beautiful if the utter agony weren't so fresh in his mind.

His legs gave out, and he fell to his hands and knees. Farren was advancing on Glenna now, and the woman spared her partner a quick glance, then screamed, "You will die, wolf. That bauble can't protect you forever."

No. He couldn't let Farren die for him. Not when he'd been the one to put her in danger in the first place. Eli dug his fingers into the sand, taking the strength he needed, and the rocks next to him started to crack and crumble. The land shook, so violently, he worried it would bring down the buildings just a few meters away, but then Glenna cried out in pain, and Farren snarled.

He couldn't believe what was right in front of him. The sand had split, opening up a crevasse between Farren and Glenna, and swallowing Monroe's body.

"You will pay for that! Both of you!" Glenna cried and directed her magic directly at the gaping maw. Sand burst into the air like someone had set off a bomb, and Farren leapt in front of Eli, shielding him with her massive body.

It was over in under a minute. The shaking stopped. Glenna was gone, and Farren was pressed against him. Her wolf took a shuddering breath, and Eli wrapped his arms around her torso. Blood coated his palm. "Fuck. You're hurt."

She shook her head, and her yip was definitely a denial. The next sound, though, that was possessive and very much the bark of an alpha wolf. She pushed at him with her front paws until he released her, then grabbed his wrist in her mouth and tugged him towards the stairs. She wasn't hurting him, not biting down hard enough to break the skin, but she was definitely *not* interested in him going anywhere other than where she had in mind.

"I'll follow, I promise," he said. His voice was hoarse, and all he wanted was to sleep for a bloody month. Well, that and to get as far from Doolin as he could.

Releasing him, she padded faster, and he struggled to keep up until she stopped at his car. "I...don't think I can drive."

She made an exasperated sound and nodded at the door. Confused, he opened it, and she hopped into the back seat, lay down, and closed her eyes. The shift started with her spine, and fuck. He'd never get used to the sound of bones cracking. Or watching her fur recede and her skin turn from dark gray to the smoothest alabaster.

In under a minute, she was naked, curled on the leather, and shuddering. "Get...in the...passenger side," she managed as she sat up. "I'll drive."

She'd drive. He didn't have to think. Or do anything but sit there and maybe rock back and forth to calm his overloaded senses.

Except when he shut the door, she was still very, very naked. The only thing she wore? The tree of life pendant the old woman had given him. In her human form, the long chain let it dangle practically down to her breasts.

Bloody hell. That's how she'd done it. Taken Glenna's power and turned it against the witch. The pendant. When Farren gunned the engine, he realized just how close he'd come to dying—or worse—and passed out.

CHAPTER NINE

reat. Eli was unconscious, his black hair plastered to his forehead, and his eyes sunken. Another five minutes and she would have been too late. The practitioners should have been able to take down the both of them easily, but before she'd shifted and left her house, Caitlin had insisted she put on the tree of life pendant.

"Why?" Farren asked. "It's a bauble. Nothing more. If it had power, it would have been able to help us with that damned book."

"Trust me. I have a feelin' about this. I'll explain more later." Caitlin eyeballed the chain. "Shift first. In case it doesn't fit."

Once Farren sat in front of Caitlin as her wolf, the air elemental knelt next to her and clasped the chain around her neck. "Now go find him. If he really is earth, we need to make sure the Thirteen never get to him."

Well, it was feckin' obvious he was an elemental. When she'd pressed herself against him on the beach, the earthquake had almost knocked both of them off their feet. And that's when she'd felt it. Sensed it. *Known* it.

Whether or not he'd known about his powers…that was still to be determined. If she found out he'd lied to her, there'd be hell to pay. But Eli wasn't just some random elemental. He'd been sent to Farren for a reason, and she'd figured out exactly what it was.

Eli was her mate. And wasn't that just like the Universe to send Farren someone she was supposed to love after she'd nearly destroyed her pack, failed in every way, and was trying to hide from a group of practitioners who wanted to kill them all.

Next to her, Eli groaned and rubbed his eyes. "Where are we going?" Sitting up straighter, he peered out the window into the dark of the evening. They were on the back roads to Farren's home, and there were no street lights here. No other cars. No houses.

"My place," she said as he turned to her and his eyes widened.

"Fuck. You're…"

"That's what happens when I shift back to this form in the middle of town with no clothing on me. Get over it."

"Get…over it?" He wrestled with the seat belt and after a couple of grunts and muttered curses, pulled off his leather jacket. "Here. Put this on."

"I'm driving, ya' arse. I don't have a problem with bein' sky clad."

"Sky clad?"

"Naked. Nude. Without clothin'." Turning down her drive-way, she felt the moment she passed through Diedre's protective wards. The pendant hanging between her breasts pulsed with power. "We're goin' inside, and ye're goin' to let me do all the talkin'. Do ya' understand?"

"No. I don't understand anything. Least of all what those two on the beach wanted from me. Or what they did to me." He winced, pressing his fist to his chest. "It still hurts."

"What does?" Concern wrapped cold fingers around her heart, and she spared him a quick glance as she parked his car around the side of the house.

"Everything. My skin. My hair. Fuck. My teeth." He hugged himself tightly, and Farren was halfway to the house when she realized he wasn't behind her.

"Dammit. I don't have time for this shite." Stalking back to the car, she yanked open the passenger door and grabbed Eli's arm to help him to his feet. He wavered for a moment, and Farren steadied him. "Eli, look at me."

His green eyes struggled to focus. "I don't know what's happening."

"Ya' almost got yerself killed by two practitioners huntin' down elementals."

"I'm not an elemental."

The eye roll might not have been a good idea given his reaction. "Ya' are. Earth. Just like Mara said. But yer power's bound somehow. Ya' used it on the beach there for a spell, then it disappeared."

"Disappeared?" His voice broke, and he shook his head. "No. This is...all too much. It isn't real."

"I'm a werewolf, Eli. Ya' saw Mara conjure fire and water from nothin'. Caitlin has air as her power. Is it so hard to believe ya' can work with the earth?" The front door slammed, and Farren cringed. "We're out of time. Shut yer mouth and let me deal with Cade and Liam, ya' hear?"

"Right. Shutting it."

This time, he followed her, his hand firmly clasped in hers, and though she felt his eyes on her body, she didn't care. This was her mate, and it didn't matter that she wanted to rip his head off his body, she'd protect him with her life.

Cade and Liam stood shoulder to shoulder in the doorway,

both of them looking like they were barely holding on to their wolves. "You brought him back here?" Cade asked. "Farren, we can't have him anywhere near Mara."

"He's not a danger to her," she said sharply. "Or to any of us. He needs our help. Now move out of the way."

"No." The two men puffed out their chests further and Liam's wolf flashed in his eyes, gold streaks amid the moss green.

"No? This is my house, in case ya' forgot. I could kick the lot of ya' out right now if I wanted." She shoved at Cade, and the alpha male took a step back. "Two practitioners just attacked him on Doolin Point Beach, and they would have taken him if I hadn't been there. So he's stayin' here, behind Diedre's wards, until we can figure out when and how his powers were bound. Now, are ya' goin' to let me inside my own feckin' house? I'd like to get dressed, and Eli needs tendin' to."

As if to prove her point, Eli toppled against her. Farren wrapped her arm around his waist and pushed through the wall the two males had formed.

"Farren. Shite," Caitlin said from the stairs. "What happened to him?" The air elemental tried to take Eli's other arm, but one look from Farren and she backed away. "Oh, my God. Ya' can't be serious."

Farren dragged Eli all the way to the third floor and into her bedroom with Caitlin following, then let him collapse onto the bed. Though she cared little about her nakedness in front of her pack—or even Cade's pack—she very much was not ready to have her mate see her like this until she knew he felt the same as she did. That he wanted her.

Tugging on a robe, she belted it tightly and sank down onto the mattress. "Will he feel it like I do?" Farren asked.

"Elementals don't have the immediate connection that our wolves do," Caitlin said quietly as she shut the door.

"But ya' did know? Eventually?"

Caitlin leaned against the wall. "I did. The first time…back in Dublin when we were young? It was a simple moment. Havin' a pint in a little pub after a rugby match. Liam put his arm around me, and it just felt…right. Like I could stay there forever and I'd never want for anythin'."

"There was a second time?" Farren brushed a lock of Eli's hair away from his face. Whatever the practitioners had done to him, he was out cold. She'd been attracted to him from the first moment they'd met. Now? She wanted to rip his clothes off. But it was more than sex. Farren ached to know him.

"There was."

Cade banged on the door. "Farren, we need to talk to you. Right fucking now."

Holding up her hand, Caitlin frowned. "I'll take care of this. At least for a wee bit." She opened the door to Cade and Liam both. "Liam, luv? Remember what happened when I came back to Seattle?"

The beta wolf's gaze softened, and he cupped Caitlin's cheek. "Of course. Ya' didn't know who ya' were, and it almost killed me."

"Not that." She let Liam take her into his arms and tipped her head up to look at him. "With Cade. When he was so mad at me for hurtin' Mara? Ya' asked for time, and he gave it to ya'. Well, Farren needs the same. She won't let Eli hurt anyone. Remember the runes I cast after she left tonight?"

"I remember ya' castin' them."

Farren knew that tone. Liam hadn't understood a thing the runes had told her. But he loved Caitlin with everything he was, and the two had developed an easy, joking way with one another the past few months.

The air elemental laughed. "Well, I'll refresh yer memory then. Farren needs to know as well."

Still sitting next to Eli, Farren draped her fingers over his.

They were cool, and in his sleep, his muscles tensed and relaxed. "Tell me, then."

"Teiwaz. The Warrior," Caitlin began. "Despite what most believe, it doesn't indicate victory in a battle with others, but in a battle with yerself. From its position, I believe Eli will ultimately be successful. He's strong, though he doesn't know it yet. Then, there was Sowelu. A rune of great power, it virtually guarantees that Eli will become his true self. He'll be able to break whatever spell or charm binds him. And finally, Gebo. A partnership. Whether it's between Eli and Farren or Eli and the rest of us, or Eli and someone else, we have to find out."

Farren wasn't certain what to make of Caitlin's casting. Or runes in general. Her mum had operated purely on instinct and science. As a member of the Garda, she'd had to. But her da'? He'd have listened to Caitlin.

"And if he partners with a practitioner?" Cade growled.

"Then I'll kill him myself." Farren stalked over to the doorway—the one Caitlin had thankfully already stepped through—and slammed the door in their faces.

She was done with their bullshit. At the moment, all she wanted to do was talk to this man lying on her bed. That and care for him. Make sure he was okay. Fuck it. She was already half gone over him, and they'd had all of three conversations?

"Wake up, ya' bastard," she whispered close to his ear. Even now, after almost dying on the beach, he smelled like the rocks and the sand and the salty air. Along with a hint of wood smoke. Strong. Solid.

She couldn't see any injuries. At least not to his well-muscled arms, his face, or his hands. But she knew all too well what magic did to a person. How it burned from the inside out. How it controlled, how it took everything you once were and reduced it to nothing but a memory.

Skimming her finger along his cheekbone, she let her wolf

take control. The animal memorized Eli's scent. The way his chest rose and fell steadily. The rhythm of his heartbeat.

Go get the first aid kit. Be ready to help him when he wakes up.

She managed to stand, but only for ten seconds. This was her mate, and her wolf refused to leave his side. So rather than do what she knew she should, Farren stretched out on the bed next to him, still fully clothed, and closed her eyes.

When her breathing matched his, she let herself drift off to sleep.

ELI

Where was he? The room was dark, but the scent…like lying in a field of heather. Floral, yet musky. The forest with a thick layer of moss after a rainstorm. His entire body hurt like he'd been flattened by a double-decker bus or run through a washing machine.

"Your powers may be bound, but you are an elemental just the same."

He wasn't an elemental. He couldn't be. Those tricks that Mara and Caitlin had done? They were just that. Tricks.

Then how do you explain what happened on the beach? Or how you've been at the epicenter of four separate earthquakes in the past two weeks?

Maybe it had all been a figment of his imagination. Perhaps he was losing his mind?

The mattress shifted next to him, and a dim light flickered on. "Awake, are ya'? About time."

Farren. Her gray eyes held concern and exhaustion as she pushed up onto an elbow.

"How do ya' feel?"

Eli looked around. He was very obviously in Farren's bedroom. A deep blue comforter rustled beneath him. Heavy curtains in the same shade hung from a burnished silver rod, and there were only a handful of personal touches scattered about. A photo on her dresser. A mug with *"In my defense, the moon was full"* in block letters. The rest of the space was clean and almost empty. Minimalist, he supposed others would call it.

"Eli?"

Her voice helped him focus. "Shattered. And confused. What happened? Why am I here?"

"Ye're here because this is the safest place for ya' right now. As for what happened...I don't know that ye're ready to hear it yet." She rose, and thank God she'd put on a robe. He had the distinct memory of her being quite naked the last time he'd seen her. "I'll get ya' some water."

When she disappeared into an attached bathroom, Eli sat up, and the room spun around him for a minute before he took a couple of deep breaths.

She didn't sit next to him. Merely handed him the glass along with a couple of painkillers and curled up in a chair in the far corner of the room.

"Those two on the beach?" he asked.

"Practitioners. They wanted ya' because ya' have earth in ya', and we killed their last one."

She sounded like she was describing the weather. *We killed their last one.* Who spoke that casually of murdering another human being? Suddenly, it didn't matter that she'd probably saved his life. That she'd taken care of him. He had to get away. Right bloody now.

"I'm going to go." As soon as he set the glass down, he was on his feet and racing for the door, but Farren beat him there and blocked his way.

"I can't let ya' do that. Not without knowin' how to protect yerself." She paused to meet his gaze. "And how to protect the rest of us."

"You can't simply keep me prisoner here." Eli reached for the door handle, but even though it turned, Farren had dug her heels into the floor, and try as he might, he couldn't budge her. Fuck. How was any woman that strong?

"Werewolf, remember?" she said with a hint of a smile. "Ya' can't best me, Eli. So ya' might as well sit down and listen."

Maybe if he truly *were* an elemental, he'd be able to take on the woman in front of him. But since that was a ridiculous notion—and even if it weren't, he had no idea how to use these supposed powers—he went back to the bed.

"Fine. Explain."

Farren rolled her eyes. "I've tried more than once, ya' know."

"I'm an elemental. I can control earth. There are practitioners who want to use me to get all four elements. Yes, you were quite clear on all of that. The problem? I don't believe you. I'm not an elemental. I can't be."

"Ya' said ya' were an orphan, yeah?" Her voice softened, and she took her seat in the chair again, snagging a soft gray blanket from the arm and wrapping it around her.

"My parents died in a car accident when I was fourteen."

"And ya' have no memory of them."

The reminder stung, even though he'd lived with the missing knowledge for more than twenty years now. "No. Vague feelings. Sometimes, I think I hear my mum's voice when I'm dreaming. But I can't know for certain."

"Elementals are born, Eli. Werewolves and vampires can be made. Practitioners study their craft, though they usually have some innate ability from birth. Fae...well, those tricky bastards sprang into existence at the beginning of everything, and they've been runnin' amok ever since."

"You think I was born an elemental. To elemental parents.

And they conveniently *forgot* to tell me?" He snorted. "They had a will. They chose the boarding school I was to attend, set up a trust to pay for University, and appointed a legal guardian."

"All that, and an accident killed them? Don't ya' think it a mite convenient that yer entire life was planned out for ya'?" She arched her brows and stared at him, daring him to contradict her.

"They were careful." Tension gathered in Eli's shoulders, and he tried to force it away. Getting angry with this beautiful and beguiling werewolf wouldn't do him any good until he got the answers he needed. And secured her promise she'd let him out of this room.

"Oh, I don't disagree with ya' there. Not a bit. They *were* careful. I think they bound yer powers when ya' were fourteen and that's why ya' have no memory of them. It's entirely possible they're still alive."

He couldn't breathe. No. No fucking way. "You have no proof of that."

"Not yet. But if ya' trust me, we could search for them. Together." Farren's mouth softened, her lips curving slightly. "Ya' came to me for a reason, Eli. Because Diedre sent ya'. And gave ya' this." Fishing the silver tree of life pendant from under her robe, she dangled it from long fingers. "This is how I saved yer life on the beach. This pretty thing absorbed one of their spells and turned it against them. Without it, I'd likely be dead, and I can't imagine what they'd be doing to ya' right now."

The memory of the blue and red lightning coursing through his body made him shudder. He'd never felt such pain or helplessness. Not even when he'd been about to drown. Or when he'd woken up in the hospital after the car accident.

"I need ya' to stay here with me because there are wards protectin' this place. Diedre created them. They hide the power of any elementals within their boundaries and stop the Thirteen from scrying for any of us. Without them, we'd be defenseless." Farren toyed with the pendant again, running her fingers over the intricate design. "Though, if we could learn more about what *this* does, we might be able to fight them."

"If I knew how it worked, or even what it was beyond a necklace, I'd tell you." He might not want to remain here in this house where several of the wolves obviously wanted him dead, but he'd started to think fondly of Farren, despite not knowing much of anything about her.

"I believe ya'." Farren rose and came to sit at the foot of the bed, just out of reach. "But there's somethin' else ya' need to know as well."

The seriousness of her tone didn't reassure him. "What?"

"Werewolves...we're instinctual creatures. Even in our human forms. As our beasts? Even more so. And when we were on that beach and yer power escaped, so did a part of ya' that I think's been buried for years."

"What does that mean?"

"Yer scent changed. From the moment ya' walked into my office, I liked how ya' smelled." Her cheeks pinked, but she held his gaze. "It's why I kissed ya'."

That kiss...he'd thought about it more than once in the roughly twelve hours since it had happened.

"So you like my soap? What does that have to do with anything?"

She chuckled, but there was little humor in it. "It's more than that, Eli. My wolf...she knows the scent of her mate. All wolves do. Lesser wolves, they can go on a tear from time to time, sleepin' around, but those of us born to lead? Alphas? Even betas? We don't. Not after we leave our twenties. Because that's when we start yearnin' to find the one destined to be ours."

"You're not making any sense." Warning bells were going off in his head. He wanted to run, but Farren was too close. She'd catch him, and when she did, he wasn't sure he had the strength to fight her. If anything, he wanted to lose himself to her.

"Ye're my mate, Eli. I didn't sense it this mornin' because ya' didn't have yer powers. But on the beach? My wolf has never been so certain of anythin' in her entire life. Ye're mine, and that means I'll die to keep ya' safe."

CHAPTER TEN

FARREN

*W*ell, shite. Her mate was looking at her like she'd just beamed down from another planet, and from her spot on the bed, she could hear his heart racing and smell his fear. That hadn't been her intention.

Yeah, and how did ya' think he'd take it?

"Oh, Farren. It's so good to hear you say that. I've been obsessed with you since the moment we met. Let's get naked and have loads of mind-blowing sex."

She snorted, which definitely wasn't the right response, because he muttered an oath under his breath and scooted back against the headboard.

"You're two sandwiches short of a picnic. Talking mates and *smelling* me and dying for me? I'll allow that the shite on the beach was magic. I've seen you shift. I know you're a wolf, and I've no reason to believe you're lying about who everyone else is and what they can do. But I am *not* an elemental, and we certainly are *not* mates."

Farren hadn't thought Eli's rejection would hurt so much. But it did.

He rolled to the other side of the bed, got to his feet, and winced, his hand pressing to the right side of his chest. "Fuck me, that hurts."

"Let me see." If the practitioners had harmed him permanently, she'd bring hell down upon them. Oh, who was she kidding? She'd do that anyway just for trying to take him from her. For trying to take him anywhere he didn't want to go.

"I don't think that's such a smart idea." He backed away from her slowly, keeping his eyes on the door the whole time.

"Oh, for fuck's sake. Stop faffin' about. Ye're my mate, yes. That doesn't mean I can't keep my hands off ya' long enough to make sure ye're not injured. The full moon isn't for another four days."

"What does the full moon have to do with anything?" He was still wary, but let Farren approach and reach for the bottom of his long-sleeved Henley.

Oh, fuck me.

The expanse of toned, bronzed muscles almost made her knees go weak—and Farren Denair would never swoon over a man. She'd sworn that years ago. A light dusting of black hair over his pects made her core clench until she focused on the deep purple bruise that spread from his shoulder to his navel.

"Ya' need somethin' for this. I've some arnica. Stay right there," she ordered and when she reached the bath, she was surprised he'd obeyed. Not that he'd get far if he tried to run. Cade's pack—and hers—would stop him. Problem was, Cade and Liam would do more than stop him.

She could only imagine the bruises he'd have if he tried to tangle with them. More than this small tube of salve could treat.

"This might be a wee bit cold." She tried to warm the arnica in her palms, but Eli still sucked in a sharp breath at her touch.

Then again, maybe that had nothing to do with the temperature of the arnica.

Do ya' feel it like I do?

She hoped to all that was holy he would. Eventually. That like Caitlin, there'd be a moment he'd *know*. Because if not, she'd have to let him go, and even the idea of it had her wolf fighting to escape.

"What are you doing?" he asked, his heartbeat erratic under her palm. "Not the arnica. What *else* are you doing? Because I want..." With a sound that could almost be described as a growl, he grabbed her around the waist and hauled her against him. His free hand tangled in her hair, and when they kissed this time, it was so much more than simply hot as hell.

Farren felt it all the way from the top of her head to the tips of her toes. She should have put something on besides her robe, because any minute now, Eli was going to be able to tell just how aroused she was.

He backed the two of them to the bed and sank down with her. Throwing her leg over his hip, she relished in the way his hard length pressed to her mound under his khakis.

Eli cupped her breast, pinching her nipple through the robe. When Farren whimpered—since when did she whimper? At anything?—he snaked his fingers under the soft flannel.

Fireworks. That was the only explanation for why she suddenly couldn't see a feckin' thing. Someone was setting off fireworks in her bedroom.

"More," she begged and palmed the steel rod just south of his belt. "Off with these."

Eli shed his pants in under ten seconds, revealing a pair of boxer briefs—oh, shite—with the moon and stars on them. If the Universe wanted to make it any clearer that this was her mate, she'd have to tattoo it directly on Eli's skin. Farren believed. But in his eyes, she saw only a healthy dose of lust. Not the depth of desire and need she felt in her own.

"Eli." Farren pressed her hand to his chest, careful not to hit his bruise. "Wait."

"I want you, Farren. Like I've never wanted anyone before. I don't understand it." He was panting now, a light sheen of sweat glistening on his brow. "I *need* you. Right bloody now."

"You think you do." Scooting off the bed, she belted her robe tighter and went to the window. With the drapes thrown open, she raised the sash and took a deep, cleansing breath of the morning air.

In two steps, he wrapped his arms around her waist, holding her back to his front. With a shudder, she braced her hands on the sill, then thought better of the position as it forced her arse to press against his erection.

"It's the matin'," she said. "Elementals don't feel it like wolves do. Not at first. It takes time. This…how badly ya' say ya' need me? That's the matin' call tryin' to get through to ya'. But all ya' have to go on is my word. And I won't have ya' givin' my wolf hope and then decidin' ya' can't give me forever. It would destroy me."

"It's just a quick shag," he said, and anger flared, bright hot, inside her. Farren whirled and shoved him, sending him flying back all the way to the bed.

"It is *not 'just a quick shag'* to me. That's what I'm tryin' to say, ya' daft bastard. My wolf? She's a part of me. As much as I'm a part of her. Two halves of one whole. We want the same things. Act on the same instincts."

God. Why couldn't her mate have been a wolf? Then he'd feel it just like she did. Instead, fate had given her an elemental —and a faulty one at that.

"I still don't understand." At least he had the decency to grab a pillow and hold it over his arousal. But all that skin…

Farren averted her eyes and ran a hand through her hair. "If we do this, we're close enough to the moon that I could bond with ya'. Even if I don't want to. If that happens…and ya' reject me, I'll never be able to settle. Never love another. Not for the rest of my life."

"Fuck me."

"Yeah." Farren stalked to the bathroom and slammed the door. She had to put some space between the two of them or she'd give in to his desire for *just a quick shag*.

She flipped on the water for the shower, then realized leaving him alone in her bedroom was a risk she couldn't take. Poking her head out of the bathroom door, she fixed him with her most commanding stare. "Do *not* leave this room. There are at least two other werewolves in this house who'd be all too happy to see ya' tied up in the basement. I'll run interference with them in a few minutes. Until then, stay put."

She didn't wait for his answer. Didn't have to. She felt it. Eli Escobar had a backbone to him, but he didn't have a death wish. He'd wait. And maybe after they talked to Caitlin and Tierney and Eli looked at the book, they'd find some answers.

***

AFTER FARREN FINISHED WASHING Eli's scent off her body, she secured her robe and found him—thankfully—fully dressed and sitting on her bed. "I sent Tierney to Doolin House for yer things. Have a shower, and he'll bring up yer luggage."

He spared her only a brief glance and a nod as he passed her.

It was better this way. With Eli angry at her, maybe she wouldn't have to battle her body's traitorous hormones constantly over the next few hours. A little space would do her some good.

She found Tierney making coffee. Exhaustion lingered in the bags under his eyes, and he was staring out into the backyard. "Did ya' have any trouble gettin' Eli's things?" she asked.

"No. Ewan kept watch while I went into Doolin House. He

said he could smell the magic, but no one followed us back here. Where do ya' want me to bring his luggage?"

"Up to my room," she said, then at his shock, added, "for now."

"So it's true." Tierney took a swig of coffee and looked her up and down. "There *is* somethin' different about ya'."

Fuck. Would everyone be able to tell? That she'd wanted to screw her mate blind? "Shut it and get his luggage. Pack meetin' in fifteen minutes. Everyone who's awake and...themselves."

"I've been stable all night," Mara said from behind Farren. "Not a single episode. Unless you could all the times the baby woke me dancing on my internal organs. And I'm pretty sure that's normal for how far along I am. At least with a werewolf baby."

Cade stood at his mate's side, flecks of silver in his steel blue eyes. "I still don't like having another elemental under this roof. But it seems to be helping her."

"Good. I'm not cookin' this morn'," Farren said. "There's enough in the cupboard to keep the lot of us from starvin' while we talk about what happens next. Someone else can haul it all to the main room." After she poured a second mug of coffee for Eli, she carried them back up the stairs, pausing outside her bedroom door.

Shite. He could be naked in there.

"Eli? Are ya' decent?" she called out.

"Enough."

What the hell did that mean? Nudging the door with her toe, she peered into her bedroom and her mouth went dry. Her mate stood in front of his open suitcase wearing nothing but a pair of black jeans. A few droplets of water clung to his broad shoulders, and she wondered what it would be like to lick them from his skin.

Get yourself under control, Farren. He's not yours. Not yet anyway.

Eli stopped with two different shirts in his hands. "Is there some sort of dress code for going to meet your doom?"

"Go with the one on the right." Farren was hopeless when it came to fashion. Most of her wardrobe was comprised of black leather pants, tanks in various shades from pale to dark gray, and her favorite motorcycle jacket. Around the house, she often donned a cashmere cardigan. One of her few indulgences.

"The persimmon? Really?" Eli asked.

"It brings out yer eyes." Why had she even noticed?

Her nipples tightened under her tank, and she set the mugs down on her dresser and hurried over to her closet. One of those cardigans would come in handy right about now.

"Is one of those for me?" Eli's deep voice sent her insides melting, and she shrugged into a super soft black scoop neck sweater Tierney had given her for Christmas the year before.

"Yeah. I thought ya' might need it. We're havin' a pack meetin' in..." she checked her phone, "less than ten minutes. We need to figure out how to unbind your elemental powers."

"I don't want to 'unbind' anything. I want to go back to London and forget any of this ever happened."

Farren flinched and almost choked on her coffee. Her mate wanted to forget her. Forget every meeting her.

"Well, that's not goin' to happen." Farren stalked towards the door, but Eli grabbed her arm. "Let go."

"No."

His touch made her believe there was still hope. He was gentle, but firm, and when he held her gaze, there was heat in his green eyes. If only she could see more. Respect. A connection.

"Eli. Whatever this is between us? It's not important now. Not when there's a practitioner who knows ye're in Doolin." She cupped the back of his neck and pulled him closer. When their lips met, electricity zinged down her spine. God. He tasted like coffee and spice, and her wolf railed against her control, desperate for the touch of her mate.

His hands skimmed down her body, cupping her arse and lifting her so she could wrap her legs around his waist. "Farren. How much longer?"

"Not long enough. Not for what I have in mind."

Shite. She was so turned on, she couldn't think straight. But if she gave in to the mating drive now, she'd regret it for the rest of her life. Because when she mated with him—*if* she mated with him—she would absolutely take her time and enjoy every bloody second.

"Put me down, ya' bastard. We have to get to the livin' room before Cade and Liam send someone up here."

Eli eased her to her feet, but he didn't seem to want to let go. "You're certain about us?"

"I'd bet my life on it. Do ya' trust me?" Farren tugged at her sweater, hoping it wasn't clinging to her breasts too much or both packs would know exactly how turned on she was.

Who was she kidding? They'd smell it on her. And she'd take no end of shite for it if Eli didn't eventually accept her.

"I don't know why..." Eli said as he shoved his feet into his loafers. "But I do."

CHAPTER ELEVEN

ELI

What was he doing walking into a room full of werewolves and two elementals who likely wanted to kill him? Despite these odd feelings he was having for Farren—feelings that made no sense as they'd known each other for only a day—he had no business being here.

He kept his hands shoved deep into the pockets of his jeans. Best not to appear a threat. Following behind Farren, he watched the subtle swing of her arse in those tight black leather pants. Did she wear anything else? He hadn't snooped in her closet, but he'd given it more than a passing thought. He wanted to *know* her in a way he'd rarely felt before.

"Did you grow up here?" he asked when they reached the second floor landing?

"No. Closer to Dublin," she said. Her voice held strain, and he reached out to snag her hand. "Don't, Eli."

They both froze. "Why not? You said we were—"

"I know what I said. And that's why. Because my wolf has

already claimed ya'. But if I'm nothin' but a 'quick fuck', then ya' could break my heart, and that's a risk I can't take. Touchin' ya? It makes me want ya' even more."

The skin of her wrist was warm and soft, and he had to force himself to release her. "Are you always this warm?" Falling into step beside her on the stairs, he made up his mind he *would* get to know her. He owed her that much for what she'd done for him on the beach, and maybe if he knew her, he'd start to feel something more than physical. Or...more than the vague fondness he already knew would never fade.

"Weres run hotter than humans by a degree or two. We also burn calories like ya' wouldn't believe." She offered him a small smile. "Ye'll see in a moment."

Eli gaped when she led him into the main room. The coffee table was piled high with bagels, packages of powdered donuts, large plastic jugs of trail mix, and a bloody *case* of dried fruit. The men each had plates piled high with food, while Caitlin and Mara's plates were more reasonably sized.

The pregnant elemental noticed him first and something in her green eyes stirred. Coppery flecks glowed for a moment and then faded. "Eli."

The lot of them turned almost in unison, and the power in their gazes...he wanted to shrink behind Farren. Or run far, far away from here. But he'd given her his word, and even if he did leave...where would he go?

"Good morning." His voice sounded odd. Like he had rocks clogging his throat. At the same time, his stomach growled, and Farren elbowed him in the side.

"Get yerself somethin' to eat. They won't bite ya'."

The fact that she'd said *won't* bite rather than *don't* bite wasn't lost on him, and he darted forward for a plate and two powdered donuts. They seemed the fastest and easiest things to take and get the hell out of the range of the two biggest wolves in the room—Cade and Liam.

Farren chose mostly dried fruit and nuts, and gestured to one of the leather chairs at the far end of the living room. He gave her a wary look, and she rolled her eyes. "Sit. I'll be right here."

Right here turned out to be perched on the arm of his chair. Her scent curled around him, and fuck. Was that...? She was aroused. He'd bet his life on it.

"Farren? Are you all right?" he whispered.

"Fine. If ya' say another thing about what I think ye're goin' to, we'll have words. Ones ya' won't like."

The threat hit him in the gut, and suddenly he wasn't hungry.

"This is my house," she said with complete and total authority infusing her tone. "But we've two packs under one roof. Not somethin' that happens often in our world. So I yield the floor to Cade with the understandin' that he's leadin' this meeting at my pleasure, and I can put a stop to it at any moment. We clear?"

One by one, each of them nodded. Though he wasn't sure he got a vote, Eli found his head bobbing as well.

The male alpha wolf took the spot in front of the darkened hearth and held his mate's gaze. "You okay, honey?"

"Fine. Having Eli here is helping me. I'm myself, Cade. I promise."

Eli wanted to know what she meant by "I'm myself," but he didn't ask. Not yet. Not with Liam staring him down like he was a stick of dynamite with a lit fuse.

"Eli," Cade said, "you bolted yesterday before we could explain the whole situation to you. Farren's vouched for you, and while I don't trust you any further than I can throw you, I *do* trust her. So I'm giving you a chance to prove you're not against us."

"I don't even know the lot of you," Eli said with his hands clasped around the plate. "I have no reason to be for or against you at the moment. I don't hurt people. I was the kid in school who got beaten up because I wouldn't fight back. Not because I couldn't, but because I don't think violence solves anything."

"If ya' stick around, ye'll have to fight." This from Tierney, the young wolf who'd brought Eli his luggage this morning. "No way around it."

For the next half an hour, Cade, Liam, Mara, and Caitlin explained the entire history of elementals and werewolves, until Eli's head started to spin. He'd managed all of two bites of donut, and eventually tried to set his plate aside, but Farren took it from him and polished off the leftovers.

"Questions?" Cade asked. "Because now's the time. Before we show you the book."

"The man's overwhelmed." Mara held out her hand, and Cade linked their fingers and sank down next to her. "Eli, I know this is a lot. When I discovered I was an elemental, Cade was trapped as his wolf and I was about to die. I was lying in bed with my arms wrapped around a wolf I had no idea was really a man, and everything was going dark and quiet. I couldn't move. The next thing I remember, I was on the floor, soaking wet, and there was a naked man in my bed." She chuckled and brushed a kiss to Cade's knuckles. "I'm sure you can imagine that wasn't the way I wanted to find out I had...abilities."

"I'd hope not," Eli said. "Not sure I would have trusted my own sanity if that had happened to me."

"I didn't. Not completely. Not until the next day when we found Livie—she's another member of our pack—and she threatened me. I drenched her with my element. Like...it was raining inside Cade's studio."

When Mara said "our pack" Cade sat up a little straighter and the look of pride and pure love in his eyes struck Eli. That was mating. Mara looked at him the same way. Shifting his gaze to Farren, he wasn't sure if he was upset or relieved that she wasn't looking at him like that. All he found in her stare was confusion and pain.

"I've seen enough to believe what you've told me," Eli began when he returned his focus to Cade. "But I still don't understand why you believe I'm an elemental too. Even if I am, I can't use whatever *powers* I might have. So there's no reason this group of practitioners—the Thirteen, yeah?—would come after me. I'd be useless to them."

"Not if they have a way to unbind yer element," Caitlin cut in. "For years, Fergus *owned* my air. When he could sense me, when I wasn't protected by the spell Mara's sister cast, my powers were...terribly weak. Almost useless. I could only call on them when *he* let me. If he didn't want me commanding the air, the best I could do was a weak breeze. Barely enough to stir the leaves on the ground."

Caitlin settled closer to Liam, and the massive man with wild reddish hair draped an arm around her shoulders.

"If whatever happened to ya'," Caitlin said quietly, "was anythin' like what Fergus did to me, ya' might not know ya' even had powers."

"Tell them about yer parents," Farren said. She rested her hand on his shoulder, and a deep sense of calm wove its way into his heart. "Or what ya' remember about them."

"Nothing." Eli reached back and gave her fingers a squeeze. Why, he didn't know. "They died when I was fourteen, and I remember nothing before waking up in hospital after what I'm told was a coma that lasted more than a week."

"Nothing. Literally nothing?" Cade asked.

"I can't tell you what they looked like, sounded like... All I have to go on is the photos from their national ID cards."

Mara rubbed a hand lightly over her belly as her brows furrowed. "Not even family pictures? Nothing in your house was familiar?"

Regret—as well as a healthy dose of self-flagellation—hit

him as he shook his head. "I was fourteen, Mara. When the barrister who'd been appointed my guardian told me that their flat had been sold and emptied while I'd been in the coma, I believed him. Didn't question a bloody thing when he dropped off a suitcase chockablock full of clothing for me but didn't bother to bring a single picture or knickknack from home. A few years later, I realized how odd that was, but by then, I'd turned eighteen."

"What about your guardian?" Cade ran a hand through his shaggy hair, frustration edging his tone. "What did he say when you asked him about it?"

Eli's cheeks felt like they were about to catch fire, but he refused to give in to the urge to stare only at his hands clasped in his lap. "He left London on my eighteenth birthday. I tried searching for him. Even hired a private investigator when I was twenty-one. He moved to Canada, then to the States, and disappeared. There's been no trace of him in more than fifteen years."

"Well, that's more than a wee bit convenient, don't ya' think?" Liam asked. The big man stood and started to pace back and forth in front of the hearth. "Caitlin, luv? Is there anythin' in that book about bindin' powers?"

"Not that we've found, but with how the letters keep shiftin' on the page, we could be lookin' at a spell for world peace or the cure for cancer and we'd never know it."

Eli peered back up at Farren. "The letters shift on the page? You're joking, right?"

"No." Farren stood, hands on her hips. "Can we all agree there's enough mystery surroundin' Eli that the likelihood of him *not* bein' a part of this whole mess is practically nil?"

One by one, the werewolves and elementals agreed.

"Then I think it's time we showed him the book."

FARREN

Every moment she spent close to her mate she wanted more. Whatever scent he was giving off, it definitely was *not* his soap, as he'd used hers today, and he still smelled like home. Like mint and spice and the woods she ran through every night. Well, except for the previous one. She hadn't been able to force herself to leave his side.

She'd rationalized it all. If she left to run, Cade or Liam would try to interrogate Eli. Or worse. But though neither of them trusted him, this was still her house, and she'd ordered him not to be harmed or disturbed. If they'd done so much as knock on her bedroom door without her around, she'd have cause to kick their arses into next week *and* throw them out of her home.

Caitlin led the way into the study, and Farren toyed with the pendant she still hadn't taken off. It was warm, and not simply from resting between her breasts. No, there was power to it, and with every step they took closer to the book, the power grew.

"What is this?" Eli asked when Caitlin opened the old, weathered tome they'd rescued from Diedre's house moments before Fergus had brought down the entire structure to get to Liam, Caitlin, and Mara.

"Every practitioner I've met," Farren said as she toyed with the necklace, "has been full of riddles and tricks. They're as bad as the Fae. Or possibly worse. At least the Fae have *some* rules they follow."

"So Diedre...the old woman who sent me here in the first place, she purposely gave you a book you can't read?" Eli shook his head. "Why do you think I can be of any help at all?"

"Because she gave you this." Farren held up the Tree of Life necklace then pointed to one of the pages with the same symbol inked in the corner. "And it's all over this damned book."

"Maybe Eli needs to be the one to hold it?" Caitlin stroked her fingers over the faded ink and glanced between the two of them. "It obviously has magic in it. Otherwise, ya' never would have been able to defeat those two practitioners last night. What if the magic's different for each person?"

Farren shrugged and loosened the clasp. Her fingers brushed Eli's palm as she passed the pendant to him, and at the contact, it was like they became one. Like they'd already mated. The connection, the burst of pure love and affection she felt for him in that moment...she'd never known its equal in all her years.

He felt it too. His green eyes glowed bright, and a low sound rumbled in his chest. Silence spread through the room, thick and oppressive, and he tightened his fingers around hers, holding on as his body started to shudder.

"What...is this?" he managed through clenched teeth.

"Mara? Give me your hand," Caitlin said. The two of them, with air, fire, and water, joined Eli and Farren, Caitlin holding Eli's free hand and Mara taking Farren's.

"I hope ya' know what ye're doin'." Fear sank like a stone in Farren's stomach, and Eli continued to shake. But now...it wasn't just him.

Books rattled on the shelves, lights swung, and the were-wolves all started to growl at once. Cade and Liam stripped off their shirts in unison, shed their pants, and dropped to hands and knees to shift. Ewan and Tierney were only seconds behind them.

"Don't hurt him!" Farren cried. This was her mate. And whatever was happening, she knew from the look on his face it wasn't his fault. Hell, he was as terrified as she was.

"I'm callin' on as much air as I can," Caitlin shouted over the roar of the whole house shaking. "Air and earth...they're two halves of one whole. Enemies and best friends all at once. Eli...whatever ye're feelin' right now? Give in to it. We're here with ya', and we'll keep ya' safe."

Farren doubted anyone would be able to keep them safe if Eli destroyed her entire house, but she focused on the connection between them and held his panicked gaze. "I've got ya', luv. Remember what I said earlier? Ye're mine, and I'd die for you."

"No, no, no," Eli moaned and squeezed his eyes shut. "I don't want to remember. None of it! Please!"

The words held so much pain, Farren almost let go, hoping to stop whatever the fuck this was. She felt his agony right along with him. Words she didn't understand sped through her mind, faster and faster until they were nothing but a blur of sound, and a band tightened around her chest, making it hard to breathe.

"Eli. Fight. Please," she panted. He was wheezing now, short, stuttering breaths that couldn't possibly sustain him for long, and Farren leaned in, still holding his and Mara's hands, and kissed him.

Ye're mine. My mate. And I'll protect ya' for the rest of my days.

She didn't know if he could hear her or even feel her, but when he broke off the kiss, he screamed her name.

The scent of the soil, of mossy earth and fresh rain and sand filled the room. Just as suddenly as it had started, the shaking stopped, and Eli crumpled to the floor.

Caitlin and Mara stood back, giving Farren space to kneel next to him. "Eli? Please say somethin', luv. I need to know ye're okay." She cupped his cheek, and though his eyes didn't open, he leaned into her touch.

"I...remember," he whispered. "Everything."

CHAPTER TWELVE

ELI

He was only vaguely aware of the chaos surrounding him. Voices. Shouting. Angry. Farren's cut through the din, and he grabbed onto it like it was all that would save him.

"Eli? Can ya' hear me? I need ya' to open yer eyes."

Can't.

His head felt like it was about to split in two. Unsurprising since he suddenly had fourteen new years of memories stuffed into his brain.

Tears burned behind his shuttered lids, and he groaned as he fumbled for Farren's hand. When their fingers intertwined, his thoughts started to clear, to sort themselves into some sort of logical order. Images came back first. His mother's smile. His father's eyes. The comic book he'd been reading when they'd come to his room, their faces somber.

Someone—not Farren—touched his forehead, and behind him, a man growled.

"Shut it, Liam. Ya' know I'm only makin' sure he's all right." Caitlin. Was Liam that much of an arse that he didn't want his mate touching another man?

"Excuse me," Mara said. "Who's the nurse here?"

"He could be dangerous, honey." The warning from Cade gave Eli the strength to force his eyes open.

"Won't...hurt anyone," he managed.

"Sorry if I don't believe you," the alpha male wolf bit out.

"Do your worst. Not sure I care any longer." As soon as he'd uttered the words, he regretted them. Farren's pain seeped through their joined hands. How in the bloody hell was that even possible?

"Well, I care," she said, angling her body between Eli and Cade as a shield. "This is my feckin' house and more importantly, *my mate*. So ya' take a step back and give the man some space."

Meeting his gaze, she sighed. "Whether ya' want me or not, Eli, I told ya'—"

"You'd protect me with your life." He pulled her down so she was practically lying on his chest and brushed his lips to her cheek. "I'm sorry, *preciosa*. I understand now. Some of it. I never meant to hurt you."

"*Preciosa*? Where did that come from?" Her words, quietly whispered in his ear, held a hint of amusement, despite the tension infusing the room.

"My father." The man had used the term all the time with his mother, and now that his memories were pinging around in his head at light speed, he picked the single word out from amid the jumble of so many more.

It was inappropriate. Farren wasn't his lover or his girlfriend or his...anything. Was she? Fuck it. She was.

"The mate bond is unbreakable."

His mother had explained love and mating to him. They'd explained so very many things that last day. Too many.

"Help me get him up and to the couch," Farren said sharply. "This floor is cold and he needs a cup of strong tea. Tierney? Ewan?"

Two sets of hands, one on each of his arms, and he was standing—though not under his own power. The werewolves half dragged him into the living room, and Liam lit a fire in the hearth while Caitlin headed for the kitchen.

He didn't want to be out here. He *wanted* to go up to Farren's bedroom. To fall asleep in her bed, surrounded by her intoxicating scent. He was too weak to manage the stairs on his own, and someone—or several someones—had already carried him up there once in the past twelve hours.

"Eli?" Farren leaned closer, concern—and something more— in her gray eyes. "What just happened?"

Clearing his throat, he tried three times to find the words but all he wanted to do was stare deep into this woman's soul and ask her how she could be so certain they were destined for one another after one single moment on that beach.

The kettle whistled, and Eli scrubbed his hands over his face, taking a moment to sort through the mess in his head.

"Can ya' sit up, luv?" Farren asked. After his nod, she wrapped her arm around his shoulders and fuck. Her scent was making parts of his body respond that he *definitely* didn't want the others to notice.

"Drink this. Earl Grey." Caitlin set a teacup and saucer in front of him, then backed away to rejoin her mate. "The binding spell is gone, yeah?"

"It is." His entire being felt...free. Different. Like his very molecules, his DNA, his cells had stretched and expanded, reformed into something new. With Farren pressed to his side, he was stronger, and staggered to his feet. "I...have to try something." With a quick glance at Cade and Liam, he continued, "I won't hurt anyone. I give you my word."

"We don't know you," Cade said. "Your word means nothing to us."

"It means somethin' to me. And since this is my house, ye'll keep back and trust him or ye'll get out." Despite her threats, there was a hint of affection in her tone. "Ye're family, Cade. All of ya'. But he's my mate." Her voice dropped to a whisper. "Whether he accepts me or not."

Bloody hell. He wanted to accept her right now, but he couldn't. Not without a whole lot more conversation and a chance for her to honestly *know* him.

Cade and Liam crossed their arms over their chests and waited, their wary expressions almost identical to one another. If he didn't think either of them could tear him apart without breaking a sweat, he'd laugh.

With Farren's arm around his waist, he headed for the french doors that opened out onto the patio. Crisp morning air brought more clarity, and he kicked off his shoes, balled his socks up inside of them, and left Farren on the flagstones while he walked barefoot onto the lawn.

Fuck me.

Power flowed from the very core of the earth. He felt it getting closer. Knew the instant it passed through the soles of his feet. His hands itched to create something. And maybe...to show off a little to the werewolves who clearly didn't trust him. Logic won out over bravado, and he flexed his fingers, knelt, and touched the ground.

The tiny tremor wouldn't rattle the most expensive crystal at Harrods, but he felt it all the same. A meter away, the thick carpet of grass split in two, and a spire of dirt rose, thinner than his index finger. The effort made his head pound, but the power was almost addicting, and he let the column grow until it was taller than he was.

Refusing to fall on his arse in front of Farren and the others, he forced a deep breath, then pushed to his feet. Using his connection with the earth to steady himself, he approached his creation, circled it, and then turned back to everyone gathered at the door.

Farren was the only one who moved, joining him at his side and taking his hand. "It's brilliant," she whispered. "But ya' know this complicates—"

"Everything." Eli threaded his fingers through her silver locks and tipped her head up so he could hold her gaze. "Do you still feel it?"

"What?"

"The connection between us. Do you still think I'm your mate?" He held his breath waiting for her answer. If she said no, he wasn't sure he'd be able to walk back into that house. Not that he had anywhere else to go.

"Yes. I'm more certain now than I've ever been. Ye're mine, Eli Escobar. No matter what power ya' have. I only have one question for ya'."

"Ask."

"Now that ya' have yer power back, what are ya' goin' to do with it?"

Twenty Years Ago

"Eli, we need you to come with us right now," his mother said with a quick backwards glance down the hall.

"I can't stop now, mum." The wet clay was so close to settling into a shape that approximated a cup, and he'd been working on the stupid thing all day. Puberty, his da' had said repeatedly. His elemental powers would be unstable for at least the next year, maybe two, depending on how quickly he "became a man," whatever that meant.

All Eli knew was that when he got angry, he'd rattle the

windows in their flat or raise a random mound of dirt in the center of the football pitch.

"You have to." The worry in her voice made him pay attention and stop the pottery wheel. His parents, both earth elementals, were the calmest, most even-tempered people he'd ever met. In his fourteen years, he could only recall a single time Mum had raised her voice, and it had been to warn him out of the way of an oncoming car.

Her light green eyes were puffy, the bags underneath swollen, and her lips pressed to a thin line.

"Hurry, son. Your father is in the basement. Clean up and go there straight away. I'll only be a few minutes behind you."

She embraced him, so strongly he couldn't breathe. "Mum, stop."

A small sob caught in her throat. "You're never too big to get a hug from your mum."

He thought he might be. Almost a man, almost able to control his power. Almost ready to apply to university. To leave home. To become...his own person, not the son his parents wanted him to be.

As he washed the clay from his hands, he regretted his errant thoughts. His parents loved him. He'd seen how his best friend James was often ignored completely by his father, and how Penny's mum hadn't been sober in years.

He gave up trying to clean under his fingernails and wiped his hands on his jeans on his way to the basement.

"Eli, sit down." Da' looked as worried as his mum had sounded, so he didn't say a word as he sank onto a stool in the center of the room. The large, mostly unfinished space was usually in complete disarray, boxes stacked haphazardly against the far wall, the drapes half open, a layer of dust covering everything.

Today, the drapes were drawn tight, and most of the boxes

were gone. When was the last time he'd been down here? A week? Two? Three?

"What's wrong?" he asked.

"There isn't time to explain, *m'ijo*. You have to trust us now." Da's eyes watered, and he swiped at them.

Was he...crying?

Mum came running down the stairs, breathless. "We have to do it now, Paulo. They're coming."

Eli sat up straighter. "Who's coming?"

Framing his face with her hands, his mum pressed a kiss to his forehead. "You are very special, Eli. And very powerful. Or, you will be one day because you have a rare gift. One even we don't understand. Take this and hold it tight."

She pressed a silver pendant into the palm of his hand.

"When the time is right, this will come back to you. And it will lead you where you need to go."

His mum and da' held hands surrounding him, and fear settled in his belly like a stone as they started to chant in a language he didn't know. Irish? Scottish? The ground rumbled under him, a breeze from nowhere ruffled his hair, and something close by started to burn. Seconds later, droplets of water fell from the wooden beams above his head, and then everything around him stopped, frozen in time.

His parents' faces held so much pain, he wanted to cry out, but he couldn't make a sound. A tear perched below his mum's right eye, unmoving, and Eli focused on it, aching to reach out and touch them, but his arms stayed glued to his sides.

The world around him shrank until it was nothing but a pinprick of light and after what felt like an eternity...that light flickered out.

CHAPTER THIRTEEN

*L*istening to Eli recount his last memories of his parents without being able to truly comfort him was the worst kind of torture. The man wasn't hers yet. Might never *be* hers.

She could sense his uncertainty. He didn't know why his parents had bound his powers or who they'd been afraid of.

"So this pendant," Farren said as she rubbed her thumb over the design, "is from them?"

"I'd never seen it before that day. Not that I can recall." Tugging on his hair like it might help jog his memory, he let out a groan. "Everything is all jumbled up in my head. Bits and pieces of my childhood, moments with my mum learning how to use my element. My da' never taught me. At least...not without her there. I don't know why."

"The last day," Mara said, "what you described sounded like they had access to all four elements. You smelled fire, felt drops of water, there was a breeze *inside* the basement, and an earthquake."

Eli nodded.

"Four elements don't just randomly appear. Either your mother, your father, or that pendant called air, fire, and water." Mara winced, and Cade immediately dropped to a knee in front of her.

"What is it, honey?"

With a huff, Mara waved him off. "She's dancing on my bladder again, and I need to pee. Stop worrying that every little twinge is something...evil."

"I can't help it," Cade muttered as she shuffled off to the bathroom. "This pregnancy is going to kill me."

"Ya' weren't there for most of Livie's," Liam added. "Ya' should have seen Shawn every time Livie complained about bein' uncomfortable or nauseous. The man lost his mind more than a few times."

Farren turned to Eli. His face was drawn, exhaustion clearly taking its toll after everything he'd been through—and it wasn't even noon yet. "Maybe ya' should rest a bit," she offered. "And I'll go into town and do some research on your mum and da'. And that barrister they left yer care to."

"I want to go with you."

"No. Not a smart idea, that. Not after what happened on the beach. The Thirteen—and I'll bet my arse those two were either members or their minions—can track elemental powers. Their use. It was one thing when yers were still bound. Quite another now that ya' have them back again."

"What would you have me do? Just stay here and hide until what? The wards wear off? Until Mara gives birth? I have a life back in London, Farren. It wasn't much of one, but it was mine. I'm not ready to simply give up on it."

His words cut deep, but the pain gave way to anger and she pushed to her feet. "No one wants ya' to give up yer life. Least of all me. But until we know more about what we're dealin' with, that's exactly what ye're goin' to do." Dropping the pendant into his lap, she turned on a heel and headed for the stairs. "Work with Caitlin and Tierney. See if ya' can make any sense of that damned book. Maybe with that talisman and another set of eyes, ye'll see somethin' that'll get ya' back to that life of yers and let me have some feckin' peace and quiet."

She fled up the stairs and flipped the lock on her bedroom door as soon as she'd shut herself inside. She wasn't one to cry over a few hurt feelings, but Eli's rejection hurt more than she imagined possible.

Her tears stopped after only a minute through sheer force of will, and she dabbed a bit of powder on her cheeks to hide the evidence, swapped the cashmere sweater for her leather jacket, and then nearly ran right into Caitlin when she opened the door.

"He doesn't understand, ya' know," the air elemental said. "What it means to find yer mate. But he will."

"He doesn't have to. I'm fine alone. Always have been, always will be." With as much bravado as she forced into her declaration, she almost believed it. Until Caitlin embraced her. "Stop it. I just fixed my face."

"Ya' can fix it again when I'm done with ya'."

Never in a century would Farren admit how good it felt to be hugged. To be cared for. Caitlin was one of the most intuitive people Farren had ever met, and she suspected the woman knew.

"He's down there tryin' to figure out what he said that made ya' so angry, and Cade and Liam are lettin' him spin his wheels a bit. It's good for our men to grovel from time to time. We can't tell them everythin', now can we?" Drawing back, Caitlin smiled. "Let Eli sit with his memories for today. By the time ya' come back from town, I suspect he'll have changed his tune about wantin' to return to that 'old life' of his. Or at least about wantin' to return alone."

"I never wanted a mate." Swiping at her cheeks, she dashed away the fresh tears and sniffled softly. "Makes ya' soft."

"It doesn't. It makes ya' stronger." Caitlin nodded towards the stairs. "Ya' see Cade and Liam every day. Do they seem soft to ya'?"

"No. But Cade needs to calm down. He's drivin' Mara batty."

Caitlin tried, unsuccessfully to stifle her laugh. "He is. But he's still the alpha of this pack. Before Peter left, ya' saw how the two of them were together. And the pack meetin' yesterday? Was there any question Cade was still very much in charge?"

"Does it matter? Eli doesn't want a mate." She had to keep telling herself that. It would make the inevitable moment when he left her easier. "I need to get to town before I say—or do—something I'll regret. Like beggin' him to come upstairs with me and get naked."

Leaving Caitlin with her mouth agape, Farren ran down the stairs and out the front door, not stopping for even a second when Eli said her name.

"Later," she called out. "Be back before dinner."

Or after. She'd stay out however long it took to get her emotions under control or find something useful about Eli's parents. Hopefully at least one of those two events would happen before the end of the day. If not...well, she'd spent the night running in the woods before. She'd just do it again.

ELI

"Leave her be, mate." Tierney, the younger of the two werewolves in Farren's pack, clapped a hand on Eli's shoulder. "When Farren needs some space, ya' best give it to her or ye'll regret it."

"She's your alpha, right?" Granted, he knew little about a

pack's power structure beyond what Farren had told him, but he wasn't sure Tierney should be talking about Farren behind her back.

"She is. We're a family, the three of us. Used to be six, but…" His blue eyes went misty until he blinked hard. "She told ya'? What happened to Colin and Brian? How Abagail disappeared too?"

He nodded.

"Farren thinks she failed us. She didn't. No one could have stopped that arsehole when he took her and Colin, and Brian… he ran off after Cade ordered us all to stay inside. Farren stopped Fergus from carvin' her up and takin' control of her, then helped Caitlin get her air back." Tierney gestured toward Farren's study, and Eli followed him. "Fergus wasn't yer average elemental," the werewolf continued. "The Thirteen branded him —like the bloke did to Colin and tried to do to Farren—and that allowed him to use some of their power."

The boy pulled an extra chair around to the front of Farren's desk for Eli, and Caitlin brought in a pot of tea and three mugs on a tray. "There's coffee too, if ya'd rather."

Eli arched his brows at the air elemental. "Coffee is for hangovers. Tea is for getting things done."

With a laugh, Tierney slapped Eli on the back lightly. "Good man. After Cade showed up with half his pack in tow, we switched to coffee every mornin'. It works well enough, but it tastes like shite."

"I wouldn't go that far." Caitlin poured the tea and sank into her own chair in front of the book. "Good coffee is the nectar of the gods."

The banter should have made him feel better, but he couldn't forget Tierney's words. "Why does Farren think she failed you? Because some crazy arse tried to kill you? How is that her fault?"

"It's not," Tierney said sharply. "It never was. But she blames herself all the same. Part of bein' a leader, I think. So when she tells ya' to stay here? She's not tryin' to be bossy."

Caitlin stifled a snort.

"Fine. Maybe she is a little," the young man said. "But she's also protectin' her mate the only way she knows how."

Her mate.

Was he? Out on the lawn, when she'd come to his side, he'd felt such an intense connection to her, it had almost knocked him off his feet. Without his element, it might have. But he didn't believe in that sort of thing. Even with the memories he now had of his father and mother.

They'd loved one another completely. So much so, they finished each other's sentences. The last day they'd had together, Mum had told him he'd one day find his mate, and that he'd know her without question. Could he say that about Farren? His heart wanted to say yes, but his head...that was a different matter.

"Eli?" Caitlin's voice brought him back to the task at hand, and he focused on the book she'd slid in front of him. The symbols made no sense to him. Dozens of letters were jumbled together. Upside down, right side up, sideways, backwards. "What is all this?"

"Sigils." Taking a notebook, Caitlin wrote a short sentence in delicate flowing script. "You make a sigil by crossing out all the vowels, then arranging the consonants in any shape you want."

"That's so bloody random," Eli said. "You could have a hundred sigils for the same damn sentence."

"Probably thousands." Tierney opened his own notebook and showed Eli page after page of a string of consonants written out like anagrams. "We've been tryin' for weeks to get through even a single page. The symbols change at random, too."

"They change?" It didn't matter how much he remembered of his parents. Of his mother using her element, of his father watching, scribbling in a little leather...notebook? Caitlin was talking now, but Eli held up his hand. "I…there's something…I need a minute. Some air."

"Ya' can't, Eli!" Tierney grabbed his arm. "The wards only protect the house, the backyard, and to the end of the driveway."

"I won't go far." He held the young man's earnest gaze. "I have to touch the earth. To feel its power."

Eli didn't protest when Tierney followed him, and thankfully, the werewolf stopped on the flagstones. Sliding his fingers between the blades of grass, Eli sent some of his power into the soil, and within seconds, a deep sense of calm settled over him.

"Paulo! Stop obsessing over those sigils and get your arse in here. Dinner's ready."

His father let out a dramatic sigh and winked at Eli. "Your mother doesn't fancy my studies. She'd rather I stick to one element and stop trying to achieve the impossible."

"The impossible?" Eli asked.

"One day, you'll understand, m'ijo. You have a strong spirit, born from the gifts of your ancestors. When you find your purpose, remember this." Eli's father clapped a hand on his shoulder and his expression sobered. "That which is written may seem like truth, but it can be reversed. If you own your power and trust your heart."

What had his father meant? If Da' had been studying sigils… could there be something else in Eli's past that would help him understand the ones in Caitlin's book?

He glanced over his shoulder at Tierney. "If I told you someone had a 'strong spirit', what would you think I meant?"

The man went white as a sheet and braced his hands on the wrought iron patio table. "Holy fuckin' shite."

CHAPTER FOURTEEN

ELI

*"Y*ou have a strong spirit. That which is written may seem like truth, but it can be reversed."

He didn't understand why Tierney and Caitlin were so agitated. "What in the bloody hell did I say?"

Caitlin patted Tierney's shoulder, though she looked a bit uncomfortable with the contact. "Sit down and find the page that changed five times in one day." Turning to Eli, she waited for him to sit down and leaned against the desk, facing him. "No one is born with more than one element. Well, no one we've ever heard of—besides Mara. She had a hint of fire in her blood for her entire life. Before she learned she was an elemental at all, the fire was slowly killing her."

"Killing her?"

"Fire and water are opposites," Caitlin explained. "They cancel each other out. Much like air and earth. Your element is stable. Solid. Mine is ethereal. Change personified. Mara wasn't using her water, so her fire was stealing the oxygen from her blood."

"Shite. But now…she has both and she's not dying. Just losing time."

Caitlin squeezed her eyes shut for a long moment. "She took her sister's element. It's almost like a split personality. Before, she had just enough fire to make her sick. Now, she has enough to take over completely."

"I still don't understand what this has to do with what my father said." His head was pounding, and all he really wanted was to see Farren.

"Yer father said you had a strong *spirit*," Caitlin said. "There aren't just four elements. There are five."

"Fuck me. What's the fifth? Aether?"

"Something of the sort," Tierney said, glancing up from the book.

"The Thirteen believe they can combine all four elements and create the fifth. The spirit. And if they're right, the person who can wield spirit could be more powerful than any other being in history." Caitlin ran a hand through her reddish brown locks. "This is all legend. But that doesn't really matter. If the Thirteen believe it, they'll stop at nothing to acquire all four elements, transfer them into one person, and see what happens."

"These dolts—the Thirteen—are bloody mad. They're doing all this on a *hunch*?" Eli couldn't believe what he was hearing. "Surely there must be some proof this is possible."

"Eli," Caitlin's tone held a hint of indulgence, like she was speaking to a child. "What if the proof is *you*?"

"Well, that would be mad. My father was earth. Just like my mum. Maybe he experimented with sigils, but that doesn't mean he was anything other than earth."

"Except for what happened when they bound your powers."

Eli replayed the memories again—not that he'd ever

completely stopped. Bits and pieces of the last moments with his parents seemed to be ever-present. His da' had been to his left, his mum to his right. Dammit. Why hadn't he paid more attention in his language classes? He'd taken Gaelic for a year at university, but hated it, so he'd not continued.

Da's voice had been stronger. And his hands...Eli had felt the heat coming from them.

"Blast it." He pushed up from the chair and stalked over to the window. "It was twenty fucking years ago. I don't understand why they had to bind my element. But what I really want to know? Why take my memories?"

Pain crept through his chest, clogged his throat, and made his headache even worse. Anger followed close on its heels. He'd lost everything. His entire identity beyond his name. All for what?

"To protect you." The air elemental joined him at the window, and a gentle breeze stirred the air. "Katerina—Mara's sister—did the same thing to me. When I didn't know who I was, Fergus couldn't find me."

"No one should have been looking for me in the first place! I was a normal kid. At least normal for being a fucking elemental." Frustration rumbled through his chest, and he spun towards the desk and slammed his hand down on a page of sigils he had no hope of ever understanding. "I can't read these any more than you can, nor will I ever be able to."

The books on the shelves rattled as a bit of his power slipped from his grasp. Fuck. He couldn't even control this *thing* he'd been born with. How the hell was he supposed to help fight a group of practitioners who could spell him within an inch of his life with just a few words?

His palm tingled, and he jerked it away from the weathered pages, cradled his hand to his chest, and started for the door.

"Oh, my God," Caitlin whispered. "Eli. Come back."

He didn't want to turn, didn't want to be reminded how useless he was. How he was trapped here until someone—not him—figured out how to guard against the Thirteen. But Caitlin's tone held such awe, curiosity got the better of him.

"What?"

When he looked down at the page, his mouth went dry. Some of the sigils were...missing. The tingling in his palm turned into heat, then pain, and he hissed, then lost the ability to draw breath completely.

Ink swirled over—or under—his skin, twisting and turning until it formed a completely new pattern. That of the pendant still in his pocket and four letters.

Caitlin grabbed his hand. "How did you do that?"

"I don't even know what I did. But it hurts like hell."

Tierney skirted the desk to join them and narrowed his eyes at the sigil blazed on Eli's palm.

"Well, that makes no sense," Eli muttered. "P-R-T-S?"

"It's missin' two letters," Tierney said. "Two I's. Rearrange the letters and ya' get spirit."

Caitlin met his gaze, her eyes wide. "Eli, whether ya' want to believe it or not, I think ya' might just be able to form the fifth element."

FARREN

Thank God for the peace and quiet of her office. For a job she knew how to do. Finding people was easy. A few hundred euros a year, along with some help from one of her mum's former Garda colleagues, and she could access the same databases as the federal government.

After an hour, she had detailed records on Eli from the moment he woke up in the hospital onwards, but nothing before then. A quick text to Caitlin—she wasn't ready to talk to her mate—and she had his birthday, but none of the male babies born on that date led anywhere. Or rather, they all led somewhere that wasn't Eli.

The barrister's name was beyond worthless, as the only mentions of him anywhere in public records were related to his guardianship. The man had no formal schooling, no license to practice law, not even a national ID card.

"His parents bound his powers *and* took his memories. The only proof his name is Eli Escobar came from this barrister," she mused as she brewed herself a pot of strong coffee. "Everything about him could be a lie."

As soon as the words left her lips, she regretted them. His name and birth date might be lies, but Eli...the person he was...that was real.

Expanding her search to include boys born within twelve months of the date he'd supplied, she combed through records until her shoulders burned and the screen started to blur.

How was it already dark outside? Seven hours? No wonder her arse hurt. She hadn't even left her chair since a little after noon. After she plugged one more set of criteria into the system and set it to run unattended, she stood and stretched her arms over her head.

"Go home. Ye're being a coward. If ya' don't talk to the man, ye'll never know if he's still plannin' on leavin'.'"

Her personal pep talk soothed her nerves, so she locked up and headed for O'Connor's. It was a good thing her fast metabolism burned off the alcohol in minutes and shifting healed most injuries or she'd be headed for liver damage from the events of the past months.

Curling her fingers around the pub's door handle, she froze at the familiar sound of spoons. Paddy sat on a bench at the end of the block, staring off into the distance.

"Twice in the same week, old man? To what do I owe the

honor?" Dropping down next to him, she waited for him to answer, but he just kept rapping those blasted spoons against his thigh. "Paddy? Are ya' all right?"

Nothing. Not even a nod. Despite how often Paddy frustrated her with his riddles and half-truths, she cared about him. More than she wanted to admit.

"Ye're scarin' me." Farren covered his hand with hers. "Shite. Ye're ice cold. Come with me. We're goin' to get some of the Irish into ya'."

He wouldn't budge when she tried to help him up, but at least turned his head in her direction. White mist swirled in his eyes, obscuring the pale blue-gray of his irises. Wrinkled lips moved silently, and Farren jammed her hands on her hips, her wolf asserting control. She felt the beast flash in her eyes, and the world around her sharpened.

The wolf could see and hear things her human form would never sense. Paddy wasn't completely silent. The faintest of whispers reached her ears.

"A boy. The promise of more. A choice was made. Regrets won't save ya'. Only trust."

"Who made the choice?" He had to be talking about Eli. What other boy was there? Paddy'd always had a knack for knowing what Farren needed, even if she couldn't understand him until it was too late. He'd always warned her. Always looked out for her in his own way.

"He's the center. The path. The light in darkness."

"Eli?"

Paddy blinked, his eyes returning to their normal color, and spots of pink rose on his cheeks. He grabbed Farren's hand, his fingers no longer frigid but almost hot. "Eliziam. Ya' risk everythin' by pushing him away, Farren."

Shock stole her words. "Did ya' just give me a straight answer?"

"Old Paddy fights. Every minute. Rarely wins. This time...he won. Go home, she-wolf. Now."

With a heavy sigh, the ancient man went back to playing his spoons. *"What was hidden will be revealed. What was never meant to exist will be the salvation of all."* His back went rigid and he uttered one final word. "Run."

CHAPTER FIFTEEN

FARREN

*S*he burst through the front door, unsure what the hell to say to her mate, and praying to all that was holy he hadn't done something stupid like make up his mind he didn't want her.

When she came face to face with him just outside her study, he looked different. Older maybe? Definitely knackered, lines of stress tight around his eyes.

"Farren." Her name came out almost as a growl, and her wolf answered with a similar sound, low in her throat.

"Ye're still here, at least." Why had she said that?

Just tell him ya' want him and get it over with.

But she couldn't find the words. Every time she tried, and she'd tested a dozen variations on the ride home, she thought about her pack. About how she'd failed them. Lost them. And how she'd fail Eli too one day. Wouldn't it be better to let him go? To send him back to his life and forget about him?

Who was she kidding? She'd never be able to forget him. Not

if she sent him away. Not if he rejected her. The animal inside her had already claimed him.

"You were clear I wasn't to leave."

Caitlin quietly shut the door behind Eli, giving the two of them privacy in the hall.

"Didn't expect ya' to listen."

There with the attitude again. Why couldn't she control it? Farren took a step closer, and Eli's scent stirred something warm inside her. Emotions she didn't want to feel.

"Afraid you're stuck with me." He held up his hand, and her heart leapt into her throat. Was he accepting the mating? She couldn't look away from his eyes until he continued. "For now."

All that hope and something she thought might be joy—it had been so long since she'd experienced that particular emotion—died with those two words, and she focused on his palm. Dark lines curved across his bronzed skin, and she frowned.

"What in the feckin' hell is that?" Grabbing his hand, she felt their bond grow, and it made her ache inside. But this—was it a tattoo?—was more important. This was shocking, and unless Ewan or Tierney had taken up a new craft in the roughly eight hours she'd been gone, *and* ordered all the equipment, ink, needles...this could only have been done by magic.

"If I knew, I'd tell you. The book and I are...linked somehow. This happens when I touch certain pages, certain symbols." Eli shook his head. "Hurts like a fucking branding iron. We were just about to stop for the day. I can't take any more."

"Any more? It's one symbol. Does it keep rewriting itself?" She traced the sigil with a finger, and only then realized Eli had changed since this morning. He'd put on a button down flannel shirt, one she recognized. "Why are ya' wearin' Liam's shirt?"

Eli stepped back, and the loss of his touch intensified the ache in her core. Until he loosened one button after another and dropped the shirt to the floor.

There wasn't a curse strong enough for the sight. His chest was covered in the dark ink. Sigils, yes. But runes as well. And other symbols she didn't recognize. "I don't know what's happening, or why. But Caitlin thinks I can use what's in the book...the parts that transfer to my skin, to become the last element. Or at least channel it."

This was too much. Farren snagged the flannel from the floor and threw it at him. "I refuse to believe that *my mate* is spirit. Caitlin's wrong. Ya' can't be."

"And why not?" Eli asked. "I don't want this any more than you do, Farren. But saying I can't be? That's a mite dismissive."

Stop pushing him away.

Paddy's words played on a loop in her head as she stared at Eli. His green eyes were brighter than they'd been just moments ago, burning with his ire, and shite. She wanted him like she'd never wanted anything or anyone else in her entire life.

"My room. Now." Turning on a heel, she marched up the stairs to the third floor, and held her door open for Eli. Not out of any desire to be kind, but to make sure he made it all the way into the room so they could have some feckin' privacy for what she had to say next.

"I deserve an apology," he said once she'd shut and locked the door. "And an explanation."

Farren wanted to rail at him. But he hadn't buttoned the shirt, and the designs across his pectoral muscles were mesmerizing. She'd thought his body was magnificent before. Now...he was somehow *more*.

"Do they hurt now?" she asked, softening her tone and placing her palm directly over his heart.

His chest heaved. "No. Only the memory of the pain is left. But I can't touch that book again today."

"Ya' don't have to. I'll speak to Caitlin if ya' need."

"I can do that myself." He covered her hand with his, holding on tight. "I meant what I said, *preciosa*. About the apology. And tack on an explanation. You ran away this morning so you wouldn't have to talk to me. Now, you're back and you're *angry.* I need to know why."

"Because if ya' truly are spirit, how will we ever be safe together? The Thirteen will come for ya'. I never wanted a mate, Eli. I don't deserve one. Not after everythin' that's happened. But here ya' are, as good as dropped in my lap, and I don't know how to react. How to get ya' to stay with me or how to let ya' go."

"I don't have any answers for you." With his free hand, he twisted a lock of her hair and tucked it behind her ear, then cupped her cheek. "But all I wanted—this entire blasted day— was to talk to you."

With that single sentence, he shattered the walls she'd so carefully built around her heart. She was an alpha. Even if she'd failed her pack, she couldn't change who she was. Part of leading was knowing which battles were worth fighting, and which she should yield. "I'm sorry. Eliziam."

"What did you call me?"

"That's yer real name. At least I think it is. Ya' weren't born Eli Escobar. Yer true name is Eliziam."

"Eliziam." The way it rolled off his tongue confirmed her guess. It sounded so natural. So very much *him.* "Why would they keep that from me?"

"It's unique. I imagine it would have led the Thirteen right to ya'." They were still connected, her hand on his chest, and Farren tipped her head up to brush her lips to his. The contact sent need straight to her core, and Eli stifled a groan. "I can't let them find ya'. Because if anythin' happens to ya', I don't know that I'd survive it."

He touched his forehead to hers with a sigh. "I wish I could tell you what you want to hear. That I feel this connection as strongly as you do."

Farren tensed, ready to pull away, but Eli wrapped an arm

around her waist and held her close. "I might. I honestly don't know. Twelve hours ago, I was a different person. But...I want to know you, Farren. Can we just...talk? Alone? Can we...for an hour or two...pretend to be perfectly boring and get to know one another?"

"On one condition. I can't *not* touch ya' right now. My wolf...she won't stand for it, and neither will I."

Eli scooped her up into his arms and in three steps, sank down with her onto the loveseat in the corner of her room. "Is this acceptable?"

"For the moment."

He settled against the cushion and draped his arm around her shoulders. "I won't let you go, Farren. I can't promise you forever. Not yet. But I can promise you right now."

ELI

They talked half the night. With every new thing he learned about Farren, he wanted more. But he was still so confused over who *he* was, he couldn't give her the one thing she wanted. A promise to stay.

It was close to 3:00 a.m. when she nodded off during a long lull in the conversation. Eli had been working up the courage to ask her about the pack members she'd lost. He'd held off, not wanting to cause her pain, but if they expected to fully trust one another, he had to hear the story from her.

Well, shite. Now what?

He didn't think sleeping in her bed was wise. Not again. Not until they'd established some ground rules. Like, no sex. Or sex only if it wouldn't seal the mating. They'd danced around the subject more than once, but Farren had backed away every time.

As gently as he could, he carried her to the bed and drew a

blanket over her. "I'll bunk on the couch downstairs," he whispered, then tiptoed out of the room and shut the door.

He'd fully intended to sleep. To stretch out and let the pain and frustration and uncertainty of the day ease from his shoulders, but the moon bathed the large expanse of yard in an ethereal glow, and he found himself barefoot in the grass, soaking up energy from the earth.

The marks on his chest stung, like fire ants were nipping at his skin, and he peeled off the shirt to find them...*moving.* "Fuck me. What now?"

His father's voice whispered in his memories. *"Air can bend the mind. Enough of it can hide even the brightest light from view."*

Brightest light. Farren had told him he'd was the light in the darkness. Or at least that's what the old man had told her.

He'd never called air before. Or fire or water. He'd never thought to try as a child. His mother had explained the four elements to him, but he was earth.

"What can the others do, Mum?"

"Don't worry about the other elements, Eli. Earth is enough. Earth will keep you safe."

"Let the boy try!" his da' said from behind him.

"No. We agreed. This is the way."

What way? What did his father want him to try?

Staring down at one of the larger symbols right over his heart, he held out his hands. The breeze stirred a lock of his hair, and he focused on the sensation. When he used his power, he only had to picture the end result in his mind. If he wanted an earthquake, he pictured the land around him shaking. The spire from this morning—or yesterday, he supposed—had been fully formed in his thoughts before he ever touched the ground.

He pictured his hair whipping about in the wind. Warmth bloomed in his chest, spreading out from his sternum. Then, the gale almost knocked him off his feet.

Fuck me. It worked.

Fire next. Mara had held it in her palm, and he tried to do the same. It took so much of his focus, his headache returned with a vengeance, but the spark was bright enough to penetrate his shuttered lids, and he shouted, "Yes!" when he saw the flame.

Last...he needed water. The wind was still swirling around him and the fire bounced and flickered in his left hand. In his right, he tried for two spinning droplets, like Mara had done.

The deluge sent him onto his arse. For several seconds that felt like an eternity, he couldn't breathe from the impact—or the shock.

Behind him, the french doors clicked open. He struggled to his feet, expecting to see Farren, but instead, found Mara walking towards him. Her eyes were wrong. No longer green, but almost blood red.

"Mara? Are you all right?"

She didn't answer, passing him silently. Like him, she was barefoot, and dressed in a pair of gray sweatpants and a loose t-shirt that flowed around her baby bump.

"I don't think you should be out here by yourself." He was a full head and shoulders taller than she was, and caught up to her easily, and when he tried to take her arm, she tensed.

"No." The hoarse word sent chills down his spine, and he jerked his hand back as a wall of water formed between them.

She wasn't just losing time. Caitlin had been right. This was a completely different woman in Mara's body.

He couldn't let her leave the property. "Help me!" he yelled at the top of his lungs, hoping to wake someone in the house.

The liquid wall followed behind Mara, and Eli prayed he had enough control to stop her but not harm her. Squeezing his eyes shut, he threw his hands forward, then drew them sharply apart, and the water split in two.

"You...cannot...stop...this..." Mara rasped, and a circle of flame rose up around her.

"Oh, I think that I can." Rain fell from the sky, dampening

the flames enough for Eli to leap over them. He wrapped his arms around Mara, pinning her hands to her sides, and lifted her off the ground, carrying her all the way back to the flag-stones just as Farren and Cade came bursting through the door.

"Get your fucking hands off my mate," Cade growled.

"I just stopped her from leaving the property," Eli snapped back, though he let go of Mara the moment Cade was close enough to hold her. "She's not herself."

"No shit." Cade kept one arm around Mara's shoulders and with the other hand, cupped her cheek. "Honey, come back to me. Please."

Farren stared at Eli, wonder and horror fighting for dominance in her gaze. "Ya' can call them all. I watched ya' from the window."

"Mara? Fight this! Fight for us, for our baby!" Cade moved his hand to her belly, and Mara sucked in a long, shuddering breath before collapsing against him. "Thank fucking God. Say something, honey."

"The spirit. It's...here," she whispered and then passed out.

CHAPTER SIXTEEN

FARREN

Cade carried Mara back inside, and as soon as the doors closed, Farren whirled on Eli. "What in the feckin' hell were ya' doin'? Callin' all four elements? At once? Do ya' have a death wish? Or are ya' just a proper idiot?"

"Pardon me? What did I do? Besides save Mara?"

"Ya' let loose so much elemental power, ya' probably lit up the world like a damn beacon! It's like ya' were *tryin'* to bring the Thirteen right to my door." She took two steps out onto the grass and grimaced. "And ya' turned the yard into a mud pit."

Eli's eyes darkened, and he held out his hand, spreading his fingers until a stiff wind came racing around the trees, and the mud hardened under her feet. "Happy now?"

"I suppose that's a wee bit better. But that doesn't get ya' out of this conversation. Ye're not alone here, Eli. This is a family, whether ya' choose to be a part of it or not, and ya' have to think about the rest of us."

"That's *all* I was thinking about." He took her by the shoulders and held her still. "If I can control all four elements, maybe I can help Mara. I only had one plan when I came out here. Find some connection with the earth so I could feel like myself again. These blasted marks on my chest started burning and then they started to *move*. They're trying to tell us something, Farren, and if I can't figure out what it is, I could lose you!"

Lose me?

"Ya' can't lose me. I'm yers. How many times do I have to say it?"

She found the answer in his eyes.

One more.

He picked her up, and Farren wrapped her legs around his waist. "Ya' can't lose me, Eli. I'm yer mate, whether ya' accept me or not."

Her back hit one of the support beams for the patio roof, and she felt his arousal pressing against her mound. She captured his lower lip between her teeth and bit down hard enough he hissed. "Sorry, luv. But ya' have to know who's the alpha here."

"Oh, really?" With only one arm supporting her arse, he had a free hand, and he pinched her nipple with surprising force, enough to make her yelp and send slick heat shooting to her core. "I can give just as good, *preciosa*."

"Show me." She'd take control later. If—or when—they mated. But for now, she could let him have this wee bit of fun.

"Will we...?" He froze, uncertainty in the line of his brows. "This doesn't seal the mating, does it? Because...shite, Farren. I want this. But forever? You deserve more than a man who couldn't keep it in his pants."

She masked the sting by glancing up at the moon. Her wolf could sense it every minute of every day, and she knew instinctually how long she had until she'd have to put physical distance between them. But the gesture allowed her to blink back a tear. "We have time. Almost two days."

"Outside or in?" He grinned, and fuck. He took her breath away. That square jaw with a hint of stubble, glass green eyes, alight with need, and those lips. Firm. Kissable.

Did she dare? To let this gorgeous man take her under the moon she loved so much? Farren pointed to the center of the expanse of grass.

Eli carried her to the exact spot and sank down to his knees. "What did you call it? Sky clad?"

"Aye. I want to see all of ya'," she said as she stripped off her dark gray tank to reveal a plain, black bra. She didn't have time for fancy lingerie. Had never seen a use for it. Under the moonlight, though, she wished she had at least something lacy.

"I'm going to peel those pants off you first."

The leather was tight enough to highlight her every curve, and Farren wriggled her hips to help him along. Eli ran his nose from between her breasts down to her panties, and the sound he made…it was something between a groan and a growl.

"Pants are off, luv. Yer turn."

Shite. His boxer briefs showed off just how hard—and big— he was. Farren skimmed her palm over the bulge, and Eli shuddered under her touch. "Do that again," he managed just before biting down on her nipple through the plain cotton until her back arched and she dug in her heels to afford him better access.

"Who's in charge here?" she asked.

"You tell me." Eli lavished attention on her other breast, and she was about ready to give in and do anything he wanted if he'd just go lower.

Her wolf flashed in her eyes, and with a burst of strength, she flipped their positions, putting Eli on his back and straddling his hips. "That a good enough answer for ya'?" Skimming her teeth along the shell of his ear, she stifled her yelp when he tugged on her panties and they ripped at the seams. "Ya' owe me another pair now."

"Start a tab. I may run up a large bill before the sun comes up."

Oh, God, she hoped he would. She wanted this man to ravage her in every way possible—after she'd done the same to him.

Running her hands over his chest, she purred, appreciating the sculpted muscles. The black lines and curves he'd absorbed from the book moved under her fingers. "Shite, Eli. The marks…"

"I can feel them. But this time, it's not pain." His voice roughened with each word, and he pulled her down to kiss her.

With command she hadn't anticipated, he demanded more, and she gave it to him, parting her lips, letting her tongue battle with his until they had to come up for air. Rolling again so he topped her allowed her to yank off his boxer briefs and wrap her fingers around his length.

"Fuck, Eli. Inside me. Now."

"Wait." With a groan, he rose to his knees. "Do we need protection?"

"Werewolves can't carry diseases. Shiftin' heals any illness. And females are only fertile on the new moon."

He pushed into her, gently at first, letting her adjust to his girth until she'd had enough with slow and careful. Digging her fingers into his arse, she pulled, hard, and he sank balls-deep in one move.

"You feel so good, *preciosa*. Like we were made for one another."

Farren cupped his cheeks to force him to meet her gaze. "We were, Eli. You're my mate, no matter what happens in the morning, and my body will always crave yer touch."

His eyes blazed with heat, but there was something new in those green depths. An emotion she refused to name, couldn't dare hope for, didn't deserve. Did he know? Or was she imagining the whole thing?

"I've never felt this way about anyone," he said quietly as he started to move his hips. "Tell me this is real."

"What does yer heart say?" Hers was already gone for him. Not exactly love. Not yet. That took time, even between mates. But something more. Something deeper. She wasn't sure if she believed in souls. In the afterlife. In a divine creator with a grand plan. But she believed in this. In Eli.

"It's real. We're...real." Eli thrust harder, and Farren canted her hips in time with his. Her body wound itself tighter, like a string on a violin, until she vibrated in perfect harmony with her mate. "I'm close, Farren."

That was all she needed to let herself go. Her climax hit hard, and the sound that escaped her lips was closer to a howl than a scream. Eli's release followed only a second behind hers, and for a single, perfect moment, they were one.

ELI

He'd underestimated the power of sex while connected to the earth. Or perhaps the difference wasn't the earth, but the woman in his arms.

"We should go in," Farren said. "Ewan and Tierney usually go runnin' around 5:00 a.m. If we're still out here then...well...I'll never hear the end of it."

Eli retrieved her tank and leather pants, but she picked up the torn panties and shook her head.

"Give me yer shirt."

He wasn't going to argue. The flannel covered everything important, but left him with the delicious view of her long, toned legs as she headed for the house. He pulled on his boxer briefs and followed, but paused at the top of the stairs outside her room.

"What are ya' waitin' for?"

"I wasn't certain you'd want me here."

Farren took his hand, and his worry faded at the touch. "We have two days." With a sigh, she corrected herself. "A bit less than two days. If ya' can't give me yer decision by then, I'll have to go. Sleep at my office until the full moon passes. It'll be too hard to be close to ya'. But I'll do it. Until then, I want this, Eli. It's the first thing I've let myself want in an age. Stay with me until we can't anymore."

She disappeared into the bath for a few minutes, and when she emerged, her hair shone in the lamplight and her skin glowed. It was her smile, though, that did him in. So much so he wondered if they really *were* meant to be.

The scent of heather filled the air as she slipped out of his shirt and settled under the blankets with him. "I like seein' ya' in my bed. If I'd slept much at all after that mess on the beach, I'd say we have another tumble, but I'm knackered. Get the light, will ya'?"

In the darkness, his words came easier, and he pressed a kiss to the top of her head. "I'm sorry for earlier. You're right. I put your family at risk. "

"Ya' did what ya' had to do." Her fingers trailed over his chest. "Werewolves can see things most others can't. Even now, with the curtains drawn and the lights off, yer markings? They're beautiful. But they're also terrifyin'. They could take ya' away from me. Or save Mara. And we won't know which until ya' test out all these new abilities." Farren angled her head so it touched his, and he relished in her warmth. "When I was twelve, I shifted for the first time. My mum warned me what to expect, but I didn't believe her. Not completely."

"It's painful, yeah?"

"Worse than most humans could ever imagine. But that's not what I meant. The power was thrillin'. So much so, I ran all night long. We lived in the countryside outside of Dublin, so it was safe. Even for a young wolf. But come mornin', I was so tired and hungry, I couldn't make it back to the house. When we're at our weakest—werewolves—the human form is easier to hold onto, so I'd shifted back, buck arse naked, twelve years old, in the middle of feckin' winter. Rainin' like it was never goin' to end, and maybe five degrees without the wind chill."

Eli pulled her closer, and she shivered in his arms.

"Mum told me not to push myself the first time, but I was at an age I didn't want to listen to anythin' she had to say. Until I'd been huddled under a tree for goin' on twelve hours, watchin' my fingers turn blue." Farren chuckled. "When she found me, she had a wool blanket, a Thermos of stew, and the sternest lecture I'd ever heard. And only after she finished did she give me the stew."

"Is this your way of telling me you forgive me?"

"It's my way of sayin' there's nothin' to forgive. Not truly. Make no mistake. What ya' did? Bloody stupid. Risky as hell. But I understand."

He was starting to think she would always understand him. No matter what he did—or failed to do. If only he understood himself.

CHAPTER SEVENTEEN

"**W**ake up, honey. You're safe. Tell me you know where you are."

"Cade?" She reached for him, her mate, her husband, her tether to reality. "It was just a dream. Right? This time? It was just a dream."

A dim light clicked on, and then Cade's arms were around her. "This time. Not…three hours ago."

"Oh, God. And Eli…Eli was there. He stopped me."

The growl rumbling in Cade's chest reassured her, despite the anger in the sound. "You went out there because of him."

"No, I didn't." She swiped at her cheeks and sniffled. "Not really. I remember some of it. Most of it, really." Settling closer to him, she rubbed her nose along his neck, a gesture she knew was asking for comfort. Reassurance. Protection.

"Tell me."

"The power woke me. He used all four elements at once, and it was like this sonic boom in my head. I didn't have time to wake you. It happened so fast. I sat up, and then everything went dark and cold and quiet. It's like that all the time at first. I'm locked in this tiny box where no light can reach me. But that only lasts for a minute. Maybe two. Then, I can see. Not well. More like…a pinhole camera. The view's distorted, but I piece things together."

Cade stayed quiet, letting her take her time. To choose her words carefully. She had to, or he'd go batshit and beg her to get an ankle monitor or something.

"Eli's powerful. More powerful than any of us. He had fire in one hand, water in another, the ground trembled under my feet, and the wind…I don't know how he was still standing. I passed him—the part of me that was in control didn't even pause—and he came after me. Called my name, tried to stop me. He did everything right, Cade. I fought him. It was strange though. I used water first. Even though fire was in control. He didn't blink at either one. Just…battled back with wind and water of his own. And then he picked me up and started carrying me back to the patio. That's when I knew."

"Knew what, honey?" He bit her shoulder lightly, holding on to let her know she was loved and very much his.

"That he can wield the last element. I felt all four of the elements align when he was holding me. It was like they clicked into place one at a time, and then…it was overwhelming. More power than I've ever felt."

"Shit. Did you…the part of you in control…*want* that power?"

Mara frowned. "No. Not at all. Whatever's making me lose time, I don't think it knows anything about the last element."

"Then what does it want?" He ran a hand through his hair, and the muscles of his chest flexed, highlighting one of the deeper scars from the time he'd spent trapped as his wolf. By her sister. He was no longer painfully thin, no longer haunted every night by the horrors her sister had inflicted on him. "Mara? Look at me."

"Sorry. I didn't go anywhere, I promise. There are just times I see you and I can't believe we found one another." She cupped his cheek, brushing her thumb over the thick stubble he'd taken to sporting since they'd come to Ireland. "I love you, Cade. I hope you know that."

His kiss rocked her down to her toes, and she was half tempted to shove all of her worries aside and let their physical connection take over to soothe them both. "I know, Mara. You're my mate. We're connected, here." He rested his hand over her heart, and she mirrored the gesture.

"There's something else I need to tell you," she said softly. "Something I didn't realize until I saw Eli out in the backyard tonight."

"What?"

"The sigils Eli took from the book, the ones that are now all across his chest? I've seen more than one of them before."

"What?" Cade sat up so quickly with her still in his arms, her stomach lurched.

"I was sixteen, I think, when my sister came to see me. She was going on and on about how she'd found the man who'd killed our mother, and that everything would be okay now. That we'd have closure, that we'd be able to move on. She was...gleeful. Like she couldn't *wait* to exact her revenge."

Cade's steely eyes darkened. "At least it took her a while. My dad got to enjoy another eight years, I think, if I have the dates right."

Mara's heart squeezed. No matter how often Cade reassured her that he didn't blame her, that she shouldn't carry even a single ounce of guilt for what her sister had done, that if anything, *he* was the one who should bear the weight since if not for his father, Mara never would have been orphaned, she still hated to see that pain in his eyes. He and his dad had been estranged for years, and she knew Cade regretted their falling out.

Rubbing her belly, she waited for their daughter to kick her hand, and she wasn't disappointed. First thing in the morning, the baby almost always responded to her touch, and the tiny impact brought her a small measure of comfort.

"Katerina left something with me. I kicked her out. Just being close to her was making me sick. But she tossed a little notebook at me before she left. I threw it away a few days later, but I peeked at a few of the pages first. It was full of sigils. I didn't know what they were at the time. The only magic I thought existed was on *Sabrina the Teenage Witch.*"

Cade chuckled and rested his hand over hers. "You know, we need to pick out some names."

"I was thinking...maybe Rachel? After your mother?"

His smile righted her entire world. If only everything could be this simple. This easy between them. If only she hadn't absorbed her sister's element—and whatever bit of Katerina came with it. Then, perhaps they'd be back in Seattle, in their house, in their bed. They'd have had dinner with the entire pack, laughing and joking and enjoying time with family.

"You need more rest, honey. Lie back down with me for a while. When everyone else gets up, tell them about Katerina's book. But until then, just stay with me."

The raw emotion in his voice was too much for her, and she wiped away another tear. "I'm sorry, Cade. I know this isn't my fault. I'm not weak because I can't fight it when the fire takes over. But I hate what this is doing to us. How we can't be...normal."

"Normal is for other people, honey. I love you, no matter what."

FARREN

The sounds of Eli's soft breaths and his strong, steady heartbeat soothed her, and she didn't want to open her eyes. If she did, they'd eventually have to get up. Out of this bed.

Here, she could pretend everything would work out. That he'd accept her as his mate, that they'd spend the rest of their lives together. That the Thirteen weren't after him—after all of them.

"Farren." The sheets rustled, and Eli draped his arm over her waist and pulled her naked body against his. A second coupling at dawn had left her muscles loose and her need partially sated, but now... Shite. She wanted him again, but he wasn't a wolf and probably needed some recovery time.

Then again, the firm pressure against her arse told her differently.

"Are ya' always this...eager?" she asked. "Not that I'm complainin'."

He stilled, and through the tentative connection they'd forged since he'd broken the binding spell, she felt an emotion she couldn't pinpoint. Rolling over, she frowned at the color darkening his cheeks. "Are ya' *embarrassed*? Why?"

"I don't have much basis for comparison." Shifting onto his back, he stared up at the ceiling. "I never had much time for dating. Only made it to the 'sex' portion of the relationship a handful of times in my life. Four? Five, perhaps? And I don't do one-night stands. Well, except for Percy. I think it was just as strange for him as it was for me."

A man?

"Ya' swing both ways, then?"

"Always cared more about the person than the parts." With a shrug, he held her gaze. "I suppose I should have mentioned that sooner."

"Why?" Pushing up on an elbow, she brushed a shock of

black hair off his forehead. "It doesn't matter to me who ya' slept with before me, Eli. What matters, is what ya' do now. Assumin' we mate. Werewolves...we're possessive to a fault. Ya' must have noticed Cade and Liam bein' overly protective of their mates."

The sound he made was almost a snort. "I did think it odd that neither Mara nor Caitlin shook my hand when we met."

"They won't touch another man unless they have to. After a year or so, we get a mite less...testy." Even now, the idea of him with another—man or woman—made her skin prickle with heat and her wolf growl deep inside. But she had no claim on him yet.

Footsteps thudded on the stairs below her bedroom, and Farren sighed. "The rest of the house is wakin' up." Her stomach rumbled, and she realized just how hungry she was. "And I need to eat. Are ya' ready to see what the day holds?"

"No." Staring down at his chest, he traced one of the bolder lines on his skin. "The very idea of touching that book again... But I have to."

"Eli—" If he didn't want to take on more pain, she'd make sure he didn't have to. The intense need to protect him, to care for him was like nothing she'd ever felt before, stronger even than her desire for him.

"Don't, *preciosa*. I have a role to play here. Of that, I'm certain." He cupped her cheek, and she bit down lightly on his thumb until he shot her a look that sobered her instantly. "And I want us to be free. Not from each other, but free to choose one another. Not because we're forced together, but because we *want* to be together."

The lump in her throat made speech impossible, but she nodded. This man was too good for her, and yet, he was here. In her bed. If he needed to be free in order to see they were meant for each other, then she'd make damn sure he was free. Today.

AFTER BREAKFAST, where Eli gaped at the sheer amount of bacon piled high on a platter alongside tall stacks of pancakes, more donuts, and several kilos of fruit salad, Farren leaned against the door jamb in her office while Caitlin and Tierney argued about what page of the book to focus on next.

"This is the page that's changed the most," Caitlin said. "Don't ya' remember? Last week, the sigils shifted every few hours."

"If they're changin' that much, they'll be harder for Eli. Physically." This, from Tierney, had Farren's back stiffening.

Eli held up his hand. "As the one suffering here, perhaps I should be making the decision? We start with the worst of it. I don't want to be dreading this page all fucking day."

Before anyone could respond, he rested both palms on the parchment, and closed his eyes. "Do it."

Caitlin placed the pendant directly over its twin symbol inked on the corner of the page.

Farren couldn't look away and had to force herself to breathe. Eli's entire body went rigid, and a low, agonizing sound rumbled in his throat. The sigils on the page started to move, twisting and turning, finally starting to spin around his hands.

The vortex on the page sped up, and her mate's body started to tremble, then shake so violently, she sprang to his side and wrapped her arm around him to keep him upright.

Power, more than she'd ever felt, more even than the pendant had absorbed on the beach, almost knocked her back, but she held on and let her wolf rise to the surface. Her skin tingled and rippled slightly. She warned her beast to stay just below the surface. She needed her human form to steady Eli, to be able to put a stop to this forcefully if it didn't end in the next few seconds.

When he collapsed against her with a groan, she half carried him over to the small couch in the corner of the room. "Eli, luv. Can ya' hear me?"

His cheeks had paled, and sweat dotted his brow. "Mine," he whispered as his head lolled against hers. "Mine."

Was he talking about her? Or something from the book? *"Mo cuishle?"*

The Irish words for my pulse—my heartbeat, my heart—came so naturally, she didn't even realize she'd said them until out of the corner of her eye, she saw Caitlin elbow Tierney in the ribs. "I told you," the air elemental hissed.

"Shut it. Both of ya'." Farren had no patience for banter or ribbing. Not when her mate still hadn't stirred. "Eli, look at me."

"Need...a minute," he managed. Fumbling for her hand, he laced their fingers and let out a heavy sigh. "Worst one. By far."

"If touchin' the feckin' book does *this* to him, we have to find another way," Farren said sharply, pinning Caitlin with a stare that was almost all wolf. "He can't keep doin' this."

"I have to. Don't ask me how I know, but I'm certain it's the only way." Eli's eyes were bloodshot and shining when Farren turned to him, but he offered her a weary smile. "There are only half a dozen more pages with the Tree of Life symbol on them. I can do this, Farren. For all of us. Just need to rest a bit in between."

If she had to watch him suffer six more times, she'd go mad. Shame, such a familiar emotion to her these days, crept up the back of her neck. One more person in her life she couldn't protect. How could she call herself an alpha? Or ever hope Eli would want her as a mate if she kept failing him?

"I can't..." Easing her hand from his, Farren rose, her legs shaking. "I can't be a part of this. Eli, please." She'd beg if she had to. Even if it was the least alpha thing she could possibly do. If it kept him safe...

Pushing to his feet, Eli straightened his shoulders, shuddered once, and stared her down. "This is my destiny, Farren. Mate or not, you don't get to tell me what I can or cannot do."

"Bloody hell, ye're all mad. I can't stop ya'. Ye're not a wolf, not my pack. Even if ya' are meant to be my family. My wolf has no power over ya' beyond whatever ya' feel for me. If ya' insist on endurin' more pain...don't expect me to watch." Turning to Tierney, she glowered at the young man. "I'm orderin' ya to keep him safe. Whatever it takes. Understand?"

"Farren, you have to believe we'd never let anythin' happen to Eli." This, from Caitlin, sent her wolf begging to be released.

"I don't know what to believe any more."

She had to get out of here. For an hour. Maybe two. Just enough time to clear her head and check on the searches she'd started last night. "I need some air. I'm goin' to town for a piece. When I come back, we're havin' a pack meetin' to find another way through this fuckin' mess."

CHAPTER EIGHTEEN

FARREN

She slammed her office door, taking a measure of satisfaction from the sound and the way the window rattled.

Stop acting like a child. Eli's an adult. And an elemental. He can take care of himself.

Farren cringed when Paddy's words came back to her. *"Ya' risk everythin' by pushin' him away."*

And yet, she'd done so. Again. Her mate. What good was she if she couldn't even trust the man who held her heart in his hands?

At least she was still a bloody good PI. And now that she had his real first name—thanks to the old man—she might be able to get somewhere with her searches.

It took less than five minutes. Only a single Eliziam had been born in the UK within three years of Eli's supposed birthday. He was four months older than he'd thought. Born Eliziam Colón to an Una Colón at a small hospital in Sheffield.

No father listed on the birth certificate. Not the real one, anyway. The fake one—the one he'd thought was genuine for twenty years—listed a Celia and Miguel Escobar as his parents.

Searching for Una Colón gave her a wealth of information. Her credit history showed lease agreements for three different flats over a period of eight years, then the purchase of a small farmhouse in the countryside not long after Eli's seventh birthday.

Farren had a few contacts in Sheffield. Leaning back so she could cross her feet on the corner of her desk, she picked up the phone.

THE PRINTER HUMMED as she transferred all she'd found to hard copies. Eli might want them, even if she'd memorized most of what she'd found.

For the past three hours, her uneasiness had grown steadily. Separation from her mate this close to the full moon was toying with her emotions, as was the way she'd left him.

Why had she been so stupid? Over the past few months, she'd been living with two other mated werewolves, and though Cade and Liam were over the top in love with Mara and Caitlin, they still had some spectacular rows on occasion. Usually for the same exact reason Farren had run from Eli today.

Eli wouldn't accept her if she didn't start trusting him.

Letting the fresh air and a rare sunny day refresh her on the ride home, she vowed she'd be better. Calmer. More supportive and less...intense.

The second she reached her living room, all those vows flew right out the window.

Eli was slumped on the couch, an arm draped over his eyes, looking like he'd been run over by a herd of elephants. His skin was downright pale, and the shallowness of his breathing sent her heart shooting directly into her throat.

"Eli! Shite. What happened?" Fitting herself to his side, she pressed unsteady fingers to his neck. His pulse was too fast, too weak for her liking, and she was about to straddle him just to get closer when he groaned softly and tried to sit up.

"I'm all right, Farren. Just knackered and with a headache the size of the Atlantic."

She believed him until she snuggled closer and rested her hand on his chest. He hissed out a breath and curled inward, and she lost the tenuous control she'd had on her temper. "Pull yer shirt up. Now."

When he made no move to do so, she did it for him and gaped. This morning, perhaps a dozen symbols, some sigils, but others quite clearly objects—the sun, the moon, a mountain range—had been scattered across his skin. Now...? His entire torso looked like a tattoo artist's life's work. Even worse? The markings continued down his sides, and she pulled him forward. "Fuck me. Eli. How did you stand this?"

His back was covered as well. The pure, raw power of all that pain hit her, and she closed her eyes so he wouldn't see her regrets over leaving him this morning. If she'd stayed, could she have prevented this? Saved him from what must have been hours of agony?

"Didn't stand for much of it." The humor in his tone set her off, and she jerked back.

"Ye're goin' to joke about this now? Tell me ye're done, at least. Give me some reason not to go tear that book into shreds and throw it into the fire."

"He's done," Caitlin called from the dining room. "And Mara just gave us an idea about how Eli can use the symbols and sigils to craft a protection spell like Diedre's."

Farren turned, shocked to see everyone else enjoying a meal while her mate was practically dead two meters away. "Ye're proud of this? Of what ya' did to him? Sittin' there eatin' while he's sufferin'?"

"Farren, I did this to myself. No one forced me. It was my choice." Eli snagged her wrist and pulled her close. "I'm not hungry. Tierney tried to get me to join them half a dozen times."

"Ya' risk everythin' by pushin' him away."

She had to trust him. Had to *show* him she trusted him or she'd lose him. But how the hell was she supposed to do that when every time she left him alone, he put himself in harm's way?

From the dining room, Liam's whisper carried. "Those two need to get on with the matin' already."

"God help us all if they don't," Cade replied.

Farren took a slow, deep breath and swallowed her angry reply, turning back to Eli instead. "Ye're truly all right?"

"I am. Better now that you're here." He settled her in his arms, and she tucked her legs under her so she could steal a few minutes of closeness with this man she was damn close to falling in love with. "Stay with me like this a while, and I'll be right as rain before you know it."

ELI

He couldn't tell Farren the truth. Not the whole of it. He hadn't moved from his spot on the sofa for almost an hour, and at one point, he'd felt his heart stutter and feared it would stop entirely.

What was worse? He still had no idea how to *use* these damnable markings. He'd been too out of it to pay attention to whatever conversation had taken place around the dining room table, and hoped Farren would ask about this idea Mara had so he wouldn't have to.

At least he'd been honest about one thing. Having Farren in his arms soothed his pounding head and his battered body. "A while" wouldn't be near long enough, though. A day, two? That would get him back to full strength.

The others joined them, couples sharing the other couches, with Ewan and Tierney bringing in chairs from the dining room. "Well, out with it," Farren said. "How is Eli supposed to use all these sigils and shite?"

Mara, a cup of tea balanced on her belly as she relaxed in Cade's arms, looked as shattered as Eli felt. She'd hovered at the edge of the study most of the morning, occasionally remarking on a particular symbol she recognized from some book her sister had given her.

"Katerina was a practitioner. And an elemental," Mara said. "The spells and charms in the fire agate pendant allowed Caitlin to hide from Fergus for years. When I was in high school, she came to see me. We weren't raised together, you know. Katerina was older when our mother was killed, and she aged out of the foster care system, while I was adopted as a baby."

As Mara explained about her sister's notebook, how some of the symbols had stayed with her, Eli watched the group gathered around him and Farren.

They were so obviously a family. Or two families, closely related. Cade hung on Mara's every word, as Liam did with Caitlin, and the mated pairs were so in sync, it bordered on the absurd.

Absurdly brilliant.

He wanted that sort of bond. To share a connection so powerful, he could feel his partner's emotions. It took until Mara had finished and Caitlin was explaining that Eli needed to find a way to activate the right symbols at the right time *while* using his elemental power that he realized the truth of it.

He already had what he wanted. Farren's uneasiness was like a cold chill along his side, yet every time he met her gaze or played with a lock of her hair or squeezed her thigh, that chill warmed until all he felt was...love? Perhaps not quite love. But close.

It only lasted for a few moments each time, and he ached to carry her upstairs and strip her naked. To tell her he needed her as much as she needed him, and that once they were free of this threat, he *did* want to be with her.

In his arms, Farren tensed, and an overwhelming sense of guilt and shame flooded him. Hers. Not his. Blast it. He had to understand why she couldn't forgive herself for what had happened to the rest of her pack. Had to see if he could find a way to prove to her she hadn't failed them.

* * *

TIERNEY BROUGHT them both cups of strong black tea, and Farren pulled a dozen folded sheets of paper from her jacket pocket. "I found a fair bit of information about yer parents, Eli. And I think I have an idea why they took yer memories along with yer powers."

He sat up a little straighter, stifling his wince when the new marks across his back pulled taut.

Farren handed him the first sheet, and he ran his fingers over the national ID photos of his mother and father. He'd forgotten so much about them. How his mother's eyes crinkled when she smiled, his father's laugh...

"Paulo Ruiz and Una Colón?"

Farren nodded. "Yes. You grew up outside of Sheffield, in a cute little cottage in the country." The second page showed a black and white picture of the home's exterior.

"Mum painted it this pale blue not long after we moved in," he said. "With trim the color of the night sky." Fuck. He missed them so much. But their last names...they didn't make any sense, and when he said so, Farren rested her hand on his thigh.

"I don't have any legitimate educational records for ya' before ya' became Eli Escobar. Only a note in Eli Colón's file about ya' being home schooled. And even that? Colón? I don't think that was truly yer mum's name. She married yer father back in Scotland, three years before ya' were born. The records from County Inverness-shire show that she took yer father's name when they wed."

"Then why did she change it when they moved? Why didn't I get his name? Or even hers?" Eli passed the papers to Caitlin and Liam, unsure how to process all of this new information. If he could just talk to them one more time, he'd know what to do.

"Oh, my God." Caitlin's tea cup clattered to the floor, the liquid seeping into the deep blue carpet. "I think I know why they did it."

"Changed their name?" Eli sat up a little straighter.

"All of it." She reached for Liam's hand, bringing it to her heart as her knuckles whitened. "The Thirteen were so angry when Fergus couldn't work the spell to take an elemental's power a second time. They compelled him to their…compound, I guess ya'd call it…and he shoved me in the boot of his car and brought me with him."

"Breathe, luv." Liam pressed a kiss to her temple. "He's gone and he'll never touch ya' again."

"I know." Her eyes held so much love for the beta wolf, and she swallowed hard and returned her gaze to Eli. "I don't know how long we were there. Days. They locked us in this dark cell underground when they weren't *punishin'* us for *failin'*."

What did this have to do with his parents? He wanted to ask Caitlin to get to the point, but the air elemental was so shaken, he kept his mouth shut.

"It must have been a full day or more," Caitlin said, "when someone finally brought us water. A man. In his mid-to-late-forties, maybe. I begged him to help me, to help us, but he shook his head. That's when I saw his eyes. They were blank. Just like Fergus's when the Thirteen compelled him."

Eli held his breath, afraid he knew exactly what she was going to say next.

"That man was your father, Eli. I'd bet my life on it."

CHAPTER NINETEEN

ELI

His father had been with the Thirteen. Even hours later, after Farren had demanded he rest—in her bed—he was still reeling. He tried to stay awake, to sift through his memories in the hopes he could find some reason—any reason—for his father to be working for the Thirteen. To be their what? Prisoner? Servant? Puppet?

Not long after the sun went down, Farren slipped into the room and lay down next to him. "I need you, *preciosa*," he whispered. Gathering her close, he ran his hands down her back to cup her arse, and she groaned.

"Shite, Eli. The moon is so close."

Their connection was the only thing holding him together. "Touching you makes me feel whole again, even though everything we learn, all the spells I try, each new mark on my body takes another piece of me."

"We have time. Until morning. No longer." Easing herself on top of him, she kissed him, offering him exactly what he needed without words. Their coupling was slow, tender, and beautiful, and Eli took his time tasting her, tracing patterns on her clit as he pumped his fingers inside her slick heat. When she keened his name, he heard so much more than her release. He heard her heart. She'd given herself over to him completely, and he suspected Farren Denair had never planned to do anything of the sort. With anyone.

After they were both spent but nowhere near sated, he drew the blankets around them while she skimmed her fingers over his chest, soothing the twinges of pain from the new markings he'd taken on this morning.

"Mara suggested we try a casting at six," Farren said softly. "The moon will be at her apex then, which could bring about extra power. We should head downstairs soon."

"I wish we could stay here. In bed. Just like this." Pressing a kiss to her neck, he relished the tiny sound, almost a whimper, that escaped her lips. "But that won't protect Mara or help me find my da'. If he's even still alive. Still…himself."

"Fergus had moments of clarity," Farren said. "Durin' the hours he worked on me, carvin' that feckin' sigil into my side, he'd swing from truly mad to almost…sane. Full of regret, knowin' exactly what he'd done—what he was doin'. If yer father was—is—under the Thirteen's control like Fergus was… all we have to do is break whatever spell they're usin' to compel him. I can't say what his mind will be like after so many years, but if he's alive, we'll free him."

Eli buried his face in her hair, inhaling her scent, memorizing it in case he couldn't give her the promise she needed in the morning. He wanted to. His every instinct was telling him to accept the mating. Caitlin had shared her story with him this morning to distract him from the pain. How she'd almost mated with Liam eleven years ago. But then Fergus had come for her. How even after Katerina had locked her memories away, given her a new name, she'd still known that something in her life had been missing. How she'd eventually found her way back to Liam.

"Elementals, we don't feel the matin' as strongly as werewolves do. But the signs are there, if ya' look for them."

"What signs?" he asked.

"Trust yer own heart, Eli. When ya' realize ya' need Farren like ya' need yer next breath, that's when ya' can be sure."

He already felt that way. Perhaps even more since learning about his father. But was that his own pain getting in the way?

"Eli?" Farren wriggled until her back was against the headboard and waited for him to join her. "I know ye're not ready. Werewolves…I told ya' how my wolf is a part of me and I'm a part of her?"

He nodded, sensing her emotions so easily. How she struggled to give him what he'd asked for when her need was almost overwhelming her.

"On the full moon, she's at her strongest, and even though I can remain in this form, her instincts are so easy to give in to. But I *can* fight them. I've a bag packed, and if we're not off to Scotland, I'll keep out of yer way. Sleep at my office or shift and let my wolf run all night long. What I'm tryin' to say is that I won't abandon ya'. Ever. For the rest of my life, I'm yers, even if ya' decide ya' don't want me."

God, he ached to tell her not to worry. That he'd mate with her and spend the rest of his life wanting her. Could he? Even without knowing what tomorrow held for either of them?

He took her hands, so much smaller than his own, and marveled at the contrast. Hers were soft, delicate, pale. His were weathered and rough from his work and carried the rich, dusky bronze of his father's skin tone. Despite being from different worlds, despite not knowing werewolves had existed three days ago, he felt more himself with Farren than he had in his entire life.

Before he could open his mouth to tell her, someone

pounded on her door. "Farren! Eli! Get downstairs," Cade called. "Peter's back."

FARREN

They scrambled for their clothes, almost tripping over one another more than once, and every time they touched, the cracks in Farren's heart opened a little wider. He cared for her. That she knew. He might even be on his way to loving her.

She was over the moon for him.

Which was why she reached for his hand before they reached the living room. Her past failures played on a loop in her head, as did Paddy's words. She wouldn't push him away. No matter the number and epic size of her past failures, this… she wouldn't screw this up.

Peter's brows shot halfway up his forehead at the sight. "I wasn't gone that long."

"Shut it. Don't take this the wrong way, but why are ya' back?" Farren asked. "I thought ya' were goin' to find a vampire in Dublin. They don't show themselves to just anyone, ya' know."

"I'm not 'just anyone,'" the scarred werewolf growled. "Regulus and I have history."

"And that would be?"

Her wolf growled, but for once, the beast wasn't demanding to be let loose or even seconding Farren's own anger. No. If the animal had a voice, she'd be telling Farren to stop giving Peter such a hard time for no good reason.

With a wave of her hand, she continued, "Sorry. That's none of my business. If ya' trust him, and Cade trusts him…"

"I don't know the man." Cade shrugged.

"I do." Liam stood and joined Peter in front of the hearth.

"He helped us when we first landed in Dublin after...after we gave up searchin' for Cade. Regulus used his *talents* to convince the O'Sullivan Foundation's Board of Directors to pull my family estate off the market so we had a place to live. For two months, he or one of his long line of progeny patrolled the grounds every night until we were satisfied no one was comin' after us."

"Talents?" Farren knew little to nothing about the creatures. Only that they survived on human blood—but blood from a creature of the *other* would also sate them.

"Vampires can, under the right circumstances, *push their own desires* into their target's thoughts," Peter said.

"Ya' mean mind control. Are ya' daft? After what the Thirteen did to Fergus? What Fergus did to Colin—and tried to do to me? Eli's father..." Farren glanced over at her mate, and the pain in his eyes? Fuck.

"Regulus owes me his life." Peter's quiet words shut down all argument. "Vampires can be evil as fuck, but they're also unfailingly honorable where a life debt is concerned. He'll never stop trying to repay me, and he'll never feel that he's been successful no matter what he does for me."

"Never?" Farren asked.

"Vampires are immortal. The rest of us? Not so much. So, he has to save my life thousands of times to repay me for what I did for him."

"Fine. Whatever. It's a damn good thing we don't take transcripts at pack meetings. We'd be on the third page already. What did he tell ya'?" She ran a hand through her hair, equal parts frustrated and intrigued.

"He's met the Thirteen. More than once. Says they're the most batshit extremist sect of practitioners he's ever met."

"That isn't news," Cade said. "What else?"

"They came—originally—from the Inverness Coven. That's the largest coven of practitioners in Europe. Thirteen members who all believed in the existence of the spirit element split off from the rest. They thought they could use spirit for good. Or...at least some of them did. Ten years later, four members had either left or had been killed. Regulus believes the remaining members—as well as their new recruits—hunted down the deserters and killed them. Or tried to. He'd heard rumors that two—Diedre and a man named Paulo—managed to escape."

Eli squeezed her hand tightly, his breath stuttering in his chest. "Paulo?"

"Yes. That name mean something—?"

"My father."

The challenge in Peter's gaze faded away, and he stared down at the floor, his hands shoved deep into his pockets. "I'm sorry, man. I didn't know."

"Did Regulus say anythin' else about Paulo?" Farren asked.

"No. I was more concerned with how to stop the Thirteen than asking about the ones that got away. He didn't know where Diedre was or offer up any information about Paulo, but he's on his way here. He had to wait until sunset to leave Dublin. You can ask him in a couple of hours."

Meeting her mate's gaze, she wanted to wrap her arms around him, offer him whatever solace he needed. But this wasn't the time. Six o'clock was approaching—too quickly for her liking—and they needed all the help they could get to keep Eli safe during whatever casting he had planned.

"Is there anythin' else? Eli's goin' to cast the protection spell in a few minutes when the moon is at her apex." Farren gave her mate's hand a reassuring squeeze, and he answered her in kind. Relief bloomed in her chest that he hadn't shut down completely at the mention of his father. God knows she might have in his shoes.

"Regulus knows where the Thirteen are, and he can take us there. Or at least show us where to go. He'll fight with us—if we want him to. The Thirteen are a threat to every creature in this world—even the not-so-living ones."

"I don't know about the rest of you," Cade said with his arm around Mara's shoulders, "but I'll take all the help we can get."

ELI

Two minutes before six, they headed outside behind Farren's house. All of them. Cade insisted that Mara stay on the patio next to him. "The last time Eli tried working with that shit, you made it almost to the tree line," he said, concern thickening his tone. "I need you to stay by my side the whole time."

She cupped his cheek and levered up on her toes to kiss him. "I'm not going anywhere, shaggy man." Turning to Eli, she offered him an encouraging smile. "You can do this."

He didn't have her confidence. Hell, he didn't even know *how* to activate the sigils that now seemed to be a permanent part of him. He felt them. All the time. Like a presence. A specter hitching a ride or a ghost tethered to him.

Farren held both his hands in the center of the expanse of grass. "I'll stay close. If anythin' feels...wrong, stop. Promise me."

"I can only tell you I'll try," he said and brushed his lips to hers. "Last night, there was a point where the elements took over, and I couldn't have stopped them for anything."

Her gray eyes darkened, the storm brewing in them full of so many emotions. Fear, concern, pride, and love. "I wish there were another way. But I know ya' have to do this."

"Farren, there's something I need you to know—"

"It's time," Caitlin said as all the wolves, including Farren, stared up at the moon. Nearly full, it bathed the yard in a warm glow, and then he stood alone. Fuck. Why hadn't he been quicker?

Stripping off his shirt and shedding his loafers, he flexed his toes until they sunk into the soil. The connection with the earth steadied him, like he was actually growing roots that extended deep underground.

With Caitlin's help, he'd been able to find names for all of the symbols Mara had remembered. Each was associated with a particular element, and so his plan was to call each element, then activate their symbol. What he didn't know how to do? Combine all four elements into spirit to complete the spell. He hoped to God once he'd gotten that far, the last step would somehow become clear.

First, he reached deep inside for the power of earth. Subtle vibrations tickled the soles of his feet. Slowly, small clods of dirt, no bigger than his thumbnail, rose and swirled around him. The ribbon of soil took on a life of its own, and he closed his eyes, picturing the massive Tree of Life spread across his shoulders. The symbol burned, only a hint of warmth at first, but then white hot, and he clenched his jaws shut so he wouldn't cry out.

If he dared look at Farren, he knew he'd find horror written across her refined features, so he kept his gaze focused on the swirling earth instead. Picturing the symbol growing tall and strong, earth's connection to spirit ready and waiting, he then turned his focus to air.

The breeze came whistling across the landscape, disrupting the flow of the earth, but Eli raised his arms, fingers splayed, commanding the two elements to move in sync with one another. Three swirls of black ink over his right pectoral muscle symbolized air, and that too, started to burn.

He wavered for only a breath when he glanced down to see the mark glowing and swallowed his terror. He could do this. The pain was only temporary. The protection spell...that could be forever.

Water came next. The droplets splashed off his cheeks, and

as they touched his skin, some hissed at the overwhelming heat. This mark was close to his left hip. Three wavy lines that ended in spirals, representing the sea. Crashing waves along a shore.

He couldn't breathe. Every time he tried, the marks burned hotter. So he called on more air, taking it within his body in an attempt to bypass his lungs. The dark spots obscuring his vision faded, and he steeled himself for his final task.

Focus. You can do this. Pain can be controlled, and when you're done, Farren will be there.

Thoughts of her gave him a burst of strength, and he summoned fire. A blazing ring flared to life around him, and the final mark, the one dead center of his chest, burst into flame.

The shock of seeing his skin burning made him falter, and he felt everything slipping from his grasp.

"No!" he cried, throwing his head back to stare directly at the moon. "I will not give in!"

No other sounds reached his ears. Just the patter of the rain, the wind's keening cry, the crackle of the flames, and the rumble of earth.

He tried to force them together, but they resisted. Fire and water hated one another, as did earth and air. His entire body was one raw nerve. The spell was going to fail. *He* was going to fail.

The trinity knot over his heart, the unification of body, mind, and soul, flared to life, but unlike the other marks, it didn't burn. Rather, it cracked, the ink snaking across his skin in rivulets. To his shoulders, down his arms, and finally, to his fingers.

Understanding dawned a moment too late. "Run!" he shouted as pure, raw power burst from his fingers. All four elements in random, rapid bursts, raced towards the trees, hedges, and the worst place of all...the house.

Wood cracked and groaned, screams and cries from the werewolves and elementals alike, then snarls, growls, barks.

End this!

The single thought was all he could manage amid the chaos, and he closed his eyes. The strength it took to ball his hands into fists left him with nothing, but before he crumpled to the ground, he felt the elements retreat, shrinking into nothingness, and taking him with them.

CHAPTER TWENTY

The weathered wood roof over the patio started to collapse, and a beam slammed into Farren's shoulder. "Fuck! Eli!"

She didn't care about the pain. She'd heal. But her mate…she had to get to her mate. The rest of the wolves scattered, Liam herding Caitlin onto the grass well away from Eli, Cade carrying Mara back into the house as a cascade of planks clipped his leg. He fell, but twisted just in time to cushion his mate's fall.

She was halfway to Eli when Ewan and Tierney—now in wolf form—bounded to her side. Fire scorched a patch of grass at least two meters square, and Eli lay in the center. His pants smoldered in places from the sparks still whirling around in the air he'd called while trying to work the spell.

"Peter!" Caitlin screamed. Farren only spared a brief glance over her shoulder. The scarred man was half buried under the remains of the porch roof, but she heard bones start to crack and his wolf's pained howl, and ran for Eli.

The smoke stung her eyes, and shite. What she wouldn't give for a little of Mara's elemental power at the moment. "Eli? Wake up, *mo ghra*." A couple of light slaps to his cheek did nothing, and Farren hauled him into her arms. Thank God for her enhanced strength. She couldn't carry him—not with how solid he was—but she could at least drag him out of the burning grass and closer to the house.

Tierney shifted back into his human form and appeared at her side. "Farren, let me take him."

"No," she snarled. She didn't want anyone touching her mate. But they couldn't just walk into the house. No. They had to clear the rubble first. Farren tried to adjust her hold on Eli, but he started to slide from her arms.

Tierney caught him easily, and Ewan, who'd also shifted into his human form, started throwing the broken pieces of wood out of the way. Liam and Caitlin joined him, while Farren could only stare at Eli, hating herself for failing to protect yet another person she loved.

The few minutes it took to clear a path to the house felt like an eternity, and Liam rushed through the narrow opening first.

"Cade! Fuck. Say somethin'!"

Caitlin was right behind him and gasped. "Where's Mara?"

Mara?

Farren took one last glance at Eli, offered him a silent apology, and followed on Caitlin's heels. The alpha wolf lay on the floor, blood oozing from a jagged cut on his forehead. His right leg was quite obviously broken and trapped under a thick beam, and Liam tossed the wood aside like it was a toothpick.

"Shift. Come on. The moon's close enough." Liam knelt next to Cade and rested his hand on the back of his alpha's head. "Ya' have to shift. Do it for Mara."

The mention of his mate's name must have been enough to

break through, and Cade groaned. Bones started to crack, and his flannel shirt split across his back as the wolf emerged. His back legs were still trapped in his jeans, and he snarled as he tore the denim to get free.

Once he stood tall and proud, he started to bark at Liam and Peter.

"I don't know. She wasn't with ya'," Liam said, sniffing the air. "Her scent's faded… How could it have faded so quickly?"

Farren hurried to the front door, catching a whiff of something foreign. Something that made her wolf snarl and whine and demand to be let free. "Magic. Someone cast a spell close by. But that's all I can smell. Not Mara. Or any other person. Just…magic."

"Caitlin," Liam said as he wrapped his big hands around his mate's upper arms. "Ya' have to stay here with Farren. The wards will hide ya'. I need to go with Cade and see if we can find Mara. Or any trace of her."

"Go." Caitlin touched the amber pendant at her throat. "We'll be fine here. I'll help Farren with Eli."

Eli. Her mate. Her unconscious, injured mate. Fuck. She should be running with Cade and Liam. Helping them. She was the strongest member of her pack, and she had a duty to this extended family she'd found herself a part of. But…Eli needed her.

"I can shift." Farren hated the weakness in her voice, the hesitation, the reluctance. "I can go with ya'. Eli…Caitlin has Ewan and Tierney to help her."

Cade's growl was a clear refusal, and Liam shook his head. "Stay with yer mate. If a practitioner has Mara—" this drew a snarl from Cade's lupine mouth, and Liam held up his hand, "—there could be more of them close by. Stay here where ye're protected. If we don't come back, ye're the only one who can find us."

Peter stripped out of his shirt. "I'm going with you."

"Hurry it up, then." With that last command, Liam dropped to all fours, letting his wolf take over. The three of them raced into the night, and Farren turned back to Tierney, who had Eli in his arms.

"Take him to my bed. Now."

Farren gave herself one minute to let her tears fall. One minute to break down and let her failure swallow her whole. She shut the front door quietly, then turned to find Caitlin at the bottom of the stairs.

"Don't just stand there. Ya' said ya' could help Eli," Farren snapped.

"I'm goin' to help you so that *you* can help Eli."

She snorted and tried to bypass Caitlin. There was no helping her. She was a terrible alpha, a worse mate, and a shite friend. The air elemental snagged her arm, and Farren growled. "Let go."

"No. I'm not a wolf, Farren. Even if I were, I'm not yer pack. So ye're goin' to listen to me for all of two minutes, and then ye're goin' to go up there and tell that man you love him."

"He'll have to wake up first." She swallowed her sob and jerked her arm from Caitlin's grip. "I never should have let him try that casting."

"That wasn't yer choice, luv. It was Eli's."

It didn't matter that Caitlin spoke the truth, or that Farren knew it. If the air elemental had the answers to life itself, it still wouldn't fix what was broken inside of her.

"Farren? Look at me. Please."

The last word swayed her, and she raised her eyes. Regrets etched small lines around Caitlin's mouth, and tears glistened on her cheeks. "I know what it's like to blame yerself. It doesn't go away no matter how many times the man ya' love tells ya' it's all right. Liam will have that limp—that terrible scar on his leg —for the rest of his life. And it's my fault. He was taken because of me. Tortured because of me. He almost died. Because of me."

"*Almost.* I got Colin, Brian, and possibly Abagail killed."

"No. Ya' didn't. I did." Caitlin faced off with Farren, her blue eyes dark as night. "Ya' want to play that game, Farren? Ye'll lose. Every time. I've enough blood on my hands to bathe this whole countryside in it. I live with that pain every feckin' day. And still...Liam loves me. Accepts me. Forgives me. Because that's what mates do. That's what *family* does. So when ya' go up there and tend to Eli, remember that. He loves ya'. I'd bet my life on it. And I know ya' love him. So get out of yer own head and *tell him that.*"

Caitlin took a step back, dashed away a tear, and gestured up the stairs. "He's waitin' for you. Go."

———

TIERNEY STOOD sentry just inside her bedroom door. "What can I do?"

"Leave us alone." She didn't spare the most loyal member of her pack more than a quick glance before climbing onto the bed next to Eli and taking his hand. Tierney had stripped off her mate's burnt jeans and covered his battered body with a sheet. Before the boy made it more than three steps, she called out, "Go get a couple of bottles of water, the good whiskey, and a handful of protein bars? Then see if there's anythin' ya' can do to help Caitlin scry for Mara."

"Aye. I will." Tierney stopped with his hand on the door knob. "He's strong, Farren. He'll come back to ya'."

"Did ya' hear that?" she asked Eli when they were alone. "Ya' have to come back to me. Understand? I don't want to live without ya'."

He didn't stir, and she slid lower, resting her hand over his heart to feel the slow, not-quite-steady beat.

"I should be angry at ya' for even tryin' that feckin' spell. And I warn ya', Eli, when ya' wake up, I will be. But until then...I'm not. Ya' were so brave, luv. And even when it all went sideways, ya' were so strong." His skin held little warmth, and Farren pulled the blankets up to cover them. "There's somethin' I want to tell ya', but I can't. Not until I can look ya' in the eyes. Ye're my mate, but what I feel for ya'…it's more than just that. Ye're everythin' I never thought I needed. Or wanted. And if ya' could wake up for me…"

Tears stung her eyes, and she reached up to stroke his hair, run her fingers through the thick locks all the way back to his ear.

Tierney slipped into the room carrying a tray and set it on the nightstand before disappearing just as quietly as he'd come.

"I broke out my best bottle of whiskey for ya'. The one I don't share with anyone unless it's a very, *very* special occasion. Like ya' wakin' up." Her words caught in her throat, and she buried her face against his neck. Hot tears spilled over, and she let herself break. For Eli. For Colin. Brian. For everyone she'd failed in her life.

It didn't matter that she was an alpha. It didn't matter how strong she was or how powerful her wolf could be. In this moment, she cared about nothing but seeing her mate's smile one more time.

ELI

The darkness trapped him like a shroud. Silent, oppressive, and deathly still. He couldn't move. Was he dead? No. Everything hurt. Even his hair. His fingernails. His dick. There wouldn't be this much pain in the afterlife. Right? Unless his first headmaster had been right and Eli had ended up in Hell.

His heart was beating though. He felt it in his ears.

Not dead, then.

The casting had gone horribly wrong. He'd tried to stop the power from consuming the house, but had he succeeded? Farren had been on the patio watching him. The roof had collapsed. Fuck. Had she gotten out?

She's a werewolf. She's strong. But...how strong?

Echoes from somewhere far away sounded like the teacher from *Charlie Brown* for all he could focus on them.

Farren?

He tried to say her name, but he was too weak, in too much pain to make a sound.

Focus on your elements.

One by one, he tried to call them. Earth, air, fire, water... Nothing. No tremors under him. No warmth. No gentle breeze across his cheeks. No water soothing his burning skin. He had to find a way out of wherever *this* was.

Eli focused on the last good thing he remembered. Farren. Her kiss. Her touch. The way she smelled—like a field of heather on a spring afternoon. On his love for her. Because he did love her. He knew that now.

He'd fix this. If he'd gotten himself into this state, he could get himself out. He just had to figure out which of the dozens of symbols he'd absorbed would bring him back.

A GENTLE CARESS tickled his cheek, and he fought against the magic trapping him in this endless darkness. How long had it been? An hour? Two? Ten? Time held no meaning in this place, but her touch gave him hope.

"Eli? Can ya' hear me?"

The words were jumbled, and it took his addled brain several seconds to rearrange them into something he could understand.

"Farrrr…..ennnn."

"Oh, God. Eli. Shite. Open yer eyes, *mo ghra*." She pressed something to his lips, and a trickle of blessedly cool water hit his dry mouth.

Open your damn eyes, fool. She's waiting for you.

Farren kissed him, and strength surged through his body. Enough for him to wrap his arm around her waist and pull her down on top of him. "Sssorry," he managed. "Did I...hurt anyone?"

Her gray eyes shone. Fuck. He had.

"Who?"

Touching her forehead to his, she didn't say anything for several seconds as guilt threatened to pull him back under again.

"Mara's missing," she whispered. "Cade got her inside before the roof fell. But he passed out, and when we got to him, she was gone."

"It's all my fault." Eli groaned as he tried to roll away from Farren, but she held him still.

"No. At least one practitioner was *in my house*. I don't know how they found us, but someone used magic to break in and either knocked Mara out or compelled her somehow. All you have to answer for is my patio. I expect something brilliant when this is all over. I'd say you owe me a sculpture of your naked body in the middle of the lawn, but, no. That's for my eyes only." She stroked his cheek, and Eli leaned into her touch.

They were meant to be together. This woman was the only one he wanted for the rest of his life. "Farren, I tried to tell you before..." The words wouldn't come. Mara's disappearance weighed on him and warred with his need for Farren.

"It's all right, *mo ghra*. I think I know." Slanting her lips to his, she took control, her tongue teasing for only a second before she broke away and skimmed her hand down his chest. "The others are downstairs. And Peter's night-walking friend should be here soon. He can tell us where the Thirteen are, and then..."

"We're going to get Mara back." Eli tried to sit up, but the room started to spin. "Shite. That casting took everything I had. I don't know if I can—"

"I'll help you." She slid an arm under his shoulders. "I'll always help you."

CHAPTER TWENTY-ONE

"Cade, sit down. Ye're goin' to wear a hole in Farren's carpet," Liam said as she and Eli joined the rest of the group in the living room. Someone—likely Ewan—had nailed thick pieces of wood over the gaping hole where the french doors had once been, and only a few pieces of plaster from the dining room ceiling still littered the floor.

The alpha wolf's snarl made Eli flinch, and he stumbled, his legs not quite stable enough to hold him. Farren braced her hand against his chest and tightened her other arm around his waist enough to keep him upright.

"Liam's right. We'll get her back." Though she wanted to believe her own words, they had to *find* the Thirteen before they had any hope of going up against them to save Mara. "How soon will Regulus be here?"

Peter gave up his seat on the sofa so Farren and Eli could sit together and checked his phone. "I'm surprised he's not here already."

"Did ya' find anythin' out runnin'?" Farren asked Liam.

"A few drops of Mara's blood at the end of the driveway. Then nothin'." With a frustrated rumble in his chest, Liam stalked over to one of the dining room chairs, spun it around, and sat with his arms crossed over the back of the thing. "It's like they made her vanish from the spot."

The knock at the front door sent Peter scurrying to the foyer. "Farren?" he called. "I need you to give Regulus permission to enter."

Glancing at Eli, she almost laughed when his expression mirrored her own question. *That's actually true?*

She didn't want to leave her mate's side, and only went far enough to peer around the corner and see a very tall, very pale man standing just outside her door. His black hair fell to his shoulders. High, sculpted cheekbones along with nearly bloodless lips gave him a decidedly *goth* vibe. Was he *trying* to fulfill a stereotype? Or was this one of those times where the fictional had been based quite literally on facts?

"Are ya' Regulus?" she asked.

"I am."

"Do ya' plan to do any bein' in this house harm?"

"I do not. You have my vow, Farren Denair. I have fed in the past day. I am sated enough to control my urges, and I wish only to provide aid. Do I have permission to enter?" His deep, smooth voice carried a hint of an accent she couldn't place. Refined, yes. But also lyrical.

"Then you may enter."

He bowed to her, then to Peter, and stepped inside.

"Living room." She jerked her head, and the vampire and Peter followed her. Yet the only footsteps she heard were Peter's. Shite. Vampires were utterly silent. No wonder they were such effective hunters.

Once Peter had introduced the vampire to everyone in the

group, Liam explained what had happened over the past five hours.

"I saw the power that one created," Regulus said with a nod to Eli. "It lit up the sky for five hundred kilometers. It is no wonder the Thirteen were able to trace it to its source."

"They found us because of the casting?" Eli asked. "Fuck me. Cade...I'm sorry—"

"Don't. Say. Another. Word." Streaks of silver and gold glowed in Cade's eyes, and he growled at Eli. "Mara and our baby could be dead because of you."

"We all agreed this was the smartest plan," Caitlin, ever the peacemaker, offered. "We need to figure out why the castin' failed."

"I wasn't strong enough." Eli's whisper made Farren's heart ache, and she twined her fingers with his.

"Ya' can't be certain of that, luv."

"The practitioner's son is correct." Every head in the room swiveled toward Regulus. His expression hadn't changed once since he'd stepped inside, his face a mask of some expression between boredom and superiority.

"Practitioner's...son?" Eli sat up with a small groan. "I'm the son of two elementals."

"No. You are not." Now, a hint of annoyance flickered in the vampire's black eyes. "Paulo Ruiz was a member of the Inverness Coven for six years before he joined the original thirteen practitioners to cleave from the mother group. Each one of them believed in the spirit element, but their reasons for doing so, their hopes, their intentions...those varied greatly."

Regulus studied Eli for a moment. "Are you certain you wish to hear this?"

"Mate, if you weren't a vampire, I'd be over there shaking you to get you to talk faster." Eli's fingers squeezed Farren's so hard, it bordered on pain. "Tell me what my father did and what the hell happened to him."

"Now wait a fucking minute." Cade's knuckles cracked as he balled his hands into fists. "Mara needs to be our priority."

"If you attempt to go up against the Thirteen without the practitioner's son claiming the power of his birthright, you will fail, and she will die." Regulus moved so quickly, all Farren saw was a black-clad blur, and then the vampire stood directly in front of Cade, close enough the alpha wolf could reach out and snap his neck. Or try to.

"And how long is that going to take? They could be torturing her." Cade's voice faltered, and he turned to Liam. "If I lose her..."

"Ya' won't, Cade. Mara's a strong one. Ya' know that. She'll fight. For herself and for yer pup." The beta wolf rose and slung his arm around Cade's shoulders. "Sit down before ya' fall down. Ye're no use to her if ya' don't rest."

"I'm not resting until she's safe."

"Stop." The single command, delivered in a tone Farren couldn't ignore, even if her life depended on it, turned her muscles to stone. Out of the corner of her eye, she could see the muscles in Eli's neck straining and his eyes darken.

Regulus cleared his throat. "This fighting accomplishes nothing. As you are now aware, I can easily glamour those within the sound of my voice. I will release you momentarily, but first, you will listen. It is close to midnight. The Thirteen were last known to be not far outside of Glasgow. I can arrange a flight for all of us and a safe place to stay. One that is well warded. I can show you to the Thirteen's stronghold. But what I cannot do is protect you between here and my home or between my home and the castle you must break into. That will require Eliziam to understand his heritage and accept his deepest fears. I suggest—though I will not use my glamour to do so—that you all sit quietly and listen."

"Let...us...go," Eli managed, to Farren's shock. How could he move? Her wolf was howling and straining against the vampire's compulsion, but getting nowhere.

"Ah. Perhaps there is hope for you yet, practitioner," Regulus said. "Not many are wise enough to find the weak point in my glamour."

Eli's free hand rested on his thigh. A strangled groan escaped his lips, and one of his fingers twitched.

"Enough. I release you."

Farren sucked in a deep, shuddering breath. "Fuck me. I never want to feel that again."

"I give you my word, Farren Denair. I will not glamour you a second time. Now that I have your attention, may I continue?"

"Hurry the fuck up," Cade ordered. "Because if I'm separated from my mate when the moon rises, I may not be able to stop myself from tearing you apart."

ELI

He didn't know what to make of this vampire. The man—creature?—was almost preternaturally still, even when he spoke.

"The Thirteen did not start out as the vile organization you know them to be. In truth, several of them wanted to use the power of the spirit element for good. They had aspirations to end war, fight disease, and spread prosperity across the lands. However, it soon became obvious that not all of them shared the same vision. A group of nine believed this power would allow them to force others to bend to their will."

Eli linked his fingers with Farren's and drew strength from the connection between them. They hadn't mated formally, and already he knew that he'd do anything for her. What must Cade be feeling right now? With a quick glance at the alpha wolf, he cringed. The man looked like he'd lost everything in the world.

"What about the others?" Farren asked.

"The remaining four protested and were marked for death," Regulus said mildly. Did the vampire feel *anything?* "Two joined with the nine rather than be killed. One man and one woman, however, refused. They fled, using what they'd learned to keep themselves hidden. The man, Eliziam, was your father, Paulo Ruiz."

Eli tightened his grip on Farren's hand enough that she hissed in his ear, "Careful, luv. I may be a wolf, but my bones do break."

Regulus shot them a look of mild irritation, and Eli whispered his apology and signaled for the vampire to continue.

"I learned all of this fourteen years ago. Rumors of the Thirteen began when they did. A quarter century has passed since their inception, and during that time, I have done my best to stay far away from them. Vampires, though some of the strongest creatures in this realm, have few protections against magic. We are very fast, can influence minds—even read them if we choose—and our memories are nearly flawless."

"How does this help us find Mara?" Cade snapped. "Or Eli's father?"

"Patience, wolf. This tale is nearly done." The vampire smoothed a hand over his sleek black hair and continued. "In my centuries of existence, I have always endeavored to stay far away from practitioners. However, I have occasionally failed in this task. Either by accident or through a rare, *unwise* decision. One of these such choices allowed the Thirteen to capture me, bind me in silver, and bring me to the place I will soon lead you. They kept me for weeks in a cell with silver bars and silver rivulets all through the walls and floor." The vampire shuddered, the only emotion he'd shown the entire time he'd been speaking, and closed his eyes for a long moment.

"I do not wish that agony on any creature. Ever. I believe I had only days left. Too weak to fight or even move, I had resigned myself to a painful, terrible end. Until shortly after nightfall, the cell door opened."

"Bloody hell. Are you pausing for dramatic effect with Mara out there somewhere?" Eli asked, pushing to his feet and swaying slightly. "Get to the fucking point."

"The man who came to my cell door was your father, Eliziam. The Thirteen had found him a few years prior. He entered my cell and offered me his wrist. His blood. He did not speak—I am not certain he could, for the Thirteen had bound him with their words and half a dozen magical symbols burned into his skin. But as I fed from him, I saw into his mind. Paulo Ruiz excelled at protection spells. He'd hidden himself, his wife, and his son for many, many years. And then one day, he was careless. I do not know what he did, only that he carried so much guilt inside of him, he believed he deserved every horror the Thirteen visited upon him."

"Shite." The strongest memories Eli had of his father were of the man's easy smile, the way he and his mother would look at one another. True love. A bond that could never be broken.

"That is an appropriate response, practitioner. I cursed many times as I strengthened. Paulo wanted to die that night. Though he could not speak, he begged me to end his life. I would have. But one of the Thirteen called for Paulo. If he had not gone to them, we would have been discovered. I gave him two drops of my blood—enough to replenish what he had given me—and used the knowledge I had taken from his mind to escape those cursed tunnels under their lair. I ran, and I have not been back to Scotland since."

"He could still be alive." A strange mix of emotions curled in Eli's gut. Hope, dread, joy, and fear. He had a chance to see his father again. To free him. But what state would the man be in? And how could Eli find the strength for another casting? Fuck. He didn't even know what he'd done wrong the last time.

"I sense your questions, Eliziam, son of the man who saved

me from a savage and horrible end. And I have answers for you. My blood will enhance your strength. With only a few drops, you will be more powerful than you could ever dream. I also know why you failed earlier tonight."

"Why?" Eli asked.

"To cast a successful protection spell, you need more than power. You need to be whole. Your heart and mind are fractured. Stuck between the world you knew and the world that is. You must make a choice. Accept everything you are—and everything you will one day be—or be doomed to failure forever."

CHAPTER TWENTY-TWO

ELI

Cade, Liam, Peter, and Ewan went to work throwing a couple of days' worth of clothes into suitcases for everyone, while Tierney, Caitlin, and Farren accompanied Eli and Regulus out to the back lawn.

The vampire bared his fangs and sank them deep into his wrist with a quiet snarl. His eyes crinkled around the edges. Pain.

Blood dripped from the wounds onto the grass, and Regulus held out his arm. "Five or six drops will be enough. Do it quickly before the wounds seal. I do not enjoy piercing my own skin."

What the bloody fuck was he supposed to do? Suck on the vampire's wrist?

His hesitation must have angered Regulus, because the vampire grabbed Eli's hair and forced his head back. Holding his arm high, he growled, "Open your fucking mouth or I will force you to comply."

Eli parted his lips, and the coppery, slightly sweet blood hit his tongue. He counted each impact, reaching seven before the vampire released him.

"Fuck me. That..." He'd been about to tell Regulus how disgusting that experience had been when a power the likes of which he'd never known surged through him. It was like every nerve ending caught fire, but there was no pain. Only an exhilaration he never wanted to end.

Regulus arched a perfectly plucked brow at Eli. "You were saying?"

"Nothing. I was saying nothing." Eli staggered away a few steps, needing a moment to compose himself before he returned to Farren's side. Because the way he currently felt? He wanted to rip her clothes off and worship her body until she begged for mercy.

Get yourself under control. If you can't cast this protection spell, people die.

That single thought sobered him, and Eli took a deep breath. He could sense *everything* now. Hear the rustle of small animals beyond the tree line to the south. Smell the rotting wood on the other side of the small stream that gurgled peacefully to the west. He could even feel the pull of the moon. Or at least, that's what he imagined this deep, tugging sensation deep in his soul was.

Turning back to Regulus, he shoved his hands into the pockets of his khakis. "I don't know how to fix whatever *fractures* you sense in my heart and mind. I've accepted my power. If I hadn't, would I have let it do this to me?" He unbuttoned his shirt to show the vampire the symbols inked into his skin. "Every single one of them felt like it was going to kill me."

The vampire gestured for Eli to follow him to the edge of the open space, then lowered his voice. "There is a matter left unsettled between you and the female wolf, yes?"

"There is. But now is a completely inappropriate time for us to strip naked and fuck like rabbits until the sun comes up." He didn't care that the vampire could likely end him without breaking a sweat. He was bloody tired of riddles and half truths and "searching for himself."

Regulus's hand shot out and wrapped around Eli's throat. "Do not make light of this situation, practitioner."

"I'm not," he croaked. "But is there some reason no practitioner on the planet can give me—or anyone—a straight answer?"

The vampire chuckled. Actually chuckled as he released his hold. "The old ways have not left much of the world. Secrecy and deception? They were necessary for survival. Practitioners were hunted and put to death. As were vampires. Werewolves. Fae."

"Your point?"

"You do not need to 'fuck like rabbits' to perform the casting." The vulgar phrase sounded so out of place coming from the vampire. "You only need to accept your flaws. And hers. And you must be willing to sacrifice all that you have, all that you want in this life, if the casting requires it."

"I don't understand. I have to be willing to mate with Farren *and* be willing to die before I get the chance? That is complete rubbish."

"It is the truth. Now try again."

REGULUS STOOD in front of Farren, Tierney, and Caitlin, ready to whisk them to safety if Eli's casting went horribly wrong once again.

How the hell was he supposed to succeed when he couldn't think of a single bloody thing to do differently?

Digging his toes into the dirt, he relished in the small tremors that started under him. Perhaps he didn't have to pull as much power as he'd done before. If he failed, at least there wouldn't be as great of a chance he'd destroy Farren's house.

The Tree of Life on his shoulders started to burn, and he balled his hands into fists. Air was next, along with her matching mark. Then water. Then fire.

Fuck. This wasn't pain. This was pure, unadulterated agony. He needed Farren. Needed her touch to soothe him.

Accept who you are. And be willing to lose everything.

Love—his love for Farren—would carry him through the worst of it. Because he *did* love her. He'd never love another. Eli pictured her in his mind as he focused on the final mark, the trinity knot over his heart. It had reformed as he'd lain unconscious in Farren's bed, and this time, when it flared to life, it glowed as bright as the moon.

"Eli!"

No. Farren, get back!

He couldn't speak. The power thrumming through him took everything he had to control, but he could see her. The air swirling around him whipped her hair back from her face, and she fought against the wind, rain, earth, and fire, taking one step after another until she was right in front of him.

"Focus, *mo ghra.* You can do this."

If she could risk everything to stand by his side, he could endure the pain a little longer. The words came to him from deep inside, even though he had no memory of learning them.

"I call upon the power of earth, air, fire, and water. Apart, they are strong. Together, they are unstoppable. Let four become one so that none of us are ever alone."

Blinding light stole his view of Farren, but he had to put all worry for her out of his mind. She was strong. She'd fight. She'd survive. Raising his hands high, he let the magic flow through them. Sparks burst from his fingers, but this time, they didn't carry the total and complete destruction from before.

Warmth wrapped around him like a blanket, and his fear

melted away. He'd been born to do this. The sigils that covered his torso pulsed, but there was no more pain. It was almost comforting. Like the marks were destined to be a part of him. He was whole now. Or...as close as he could be until the full moon.

A ring of light hovered above his palms, and he held it, turned it over and over again, stretched it and compressed it again, until he knew what to do.

Blinking hard, he focused on Farren. "This...will protect you, my mate." He held out his hand, and when she placed her fingers in his, he sent the light into her.

Farren gasped and pressed her free hand to her heart. "What did you just do?"

With a snap, he created a second ring, then a third, and a fourth. "Get everyone out here. I don't know how long I can hold this."

One by one, the wolves and elementals appeared in front of him. Eli passed the charm on to each one of them in turn, and when he'd finished, he only wavered for a minute before the magic fell away and he was in Farren's arms.

"Ya' did it, *mo ghra.*" Farren kissed him, and suddenly nothing else mattered. He'd given his new family a fighting chance.

CHAPTER TWENTY-THREE

FARREN

She could feel the full moon approaching as the plane touched down at a private airfield not far from Glasgow. One advantage to having a centuries-old vampire among your group? They generally had more money than they knew what to do with, and thus...all the fanciest toys. Like this plane.

There was even a private bedroom in the back, and more than once she'd thought about asking if she and Eli could nip back there to seal the mating. But one look at Cade, and she'd written the idea off as not only foolish, but completely inappropriate.

The man was in so much pain, he couldn't see straight.

"Cade?" Farren approached him warily. He'd spent the two-hour flight with his fingers digging deep into the armrests of the plush leather seat, his eyes closed, the occasional low growl coming from his lips. "We're here."

The look in his eyes when he stared up at her shattered her heart into pieces. "I can't feel her. I could always feel her...even if we were apart. I couldn't sense her emotions over a distance, but just knowing she was there... Now, it's like she's gone."

"They're just hidin' her. I know it." Dropping to a knee next to his seat, Farren clasped her hands on her thigh. "When Fergus had me, I couldn't feel the moon. If Eli can hide us from their spells, it's just as likely they can hide themselves from anythin' we might do to find them."

Regulus came up behind her without a sound, but she sensed his presence. "Farren is correct. You cannot be certain of anything where the Thirteen are concerned."

Liam cleared his throat. "We'll find her, Cade. None of us will rest until she's safe. Ya' know that. She's ours, and we'll die before we give up on her." The beta wolf held out his hand, and Cade clasped it, letting Liam pull him to his feet.

"I won't survive losing her."

"Then ya' won't lose her." Jerking his head towards the stairs, Liam waited for Cade to exit the plane before following. One by one, the other wolves and Caitlin trailed behind until finally, only Farren, Eli, and the vampire were left.

"I must speak with you both, privately," Regulus said. "Where we are going...even the land carries strong, dark magic. The protection spells Eliziam cast will only hide us until we pass through the Thirteen's wards. After that, we are vulnerable."

"Is this supposed to be a pep talk?" Eli asked. "Because it's a terrible one."

"No. This is a warning. Do not let your guard down for a single second. I will protect you until I can fight no more, Eliziam, for I owe your father a life debt. I offer your mate the same."

"It feels like ye're tellin' us we're doomed to fail." Farren took Eli's hand, drawing strength from his touch.

"We are. I am very old, she-wolf. I have been alive for more than three centuries, and I have seen many creatures go up against practitioners and fail. Even the Fae, and they are the most devious tricksters to ever walk this earth. If any of us escape with our lives, it will be—and I do not use this word lightly—a miracle."

"Have ya' ever seen someone like Eli fight them?" Farren asked. Her mate was strong. Stronger than even he knew. Farren could sense his power every time they touched.

Regulus inclined his head. "No. I have not. But Eliziam's talents mean nothing if he is not whole." Leaning close enough for Farren to get a whiff of the vampire's scent—cloves and tobacco and blood—he held her gaze. In her head, his words boomed like a thunderstorm.

He will need you before the end, Farren Denair. If you cannot forgive yourself, you will fail, and that will be the end of us all.

The truth of the vampire's words hit her like a hammer, and she let go of her mate's hand. Forgive herself? She couldn't. She'd gotten her beta, one of her oldest friends, killed. Lost two other wolves, one to Fergus and the other...well, she doubted she'd ever know where Abagail went off to. And she was supposed to simply...let go of that pain?

"Ye're a proper bastard, Regulus," she hissed. "And ya' better be wrong."

The night walker straightened his shoulders and stared down his sharp nose at her. "I am never wrong."

ELI

The vampire had three cars ready and waiting for them, one with heavily tinted windows.

"I cannot walk in the sun under normal conditions. But I have a way to do so today for a very short time," Regulus said as he revved the engine and peeled out with a squeal of tires. "The year was 1888, and I was in London. In the middle of the night,

I heard a woman scream. I feed from humans, of course, but I do not kill them unless I must. I found her in an alley as a vile, disgusting creature hacked away at her body with a large knife. The Ripper died at my hand, and the woman...I gave her a choice. I could not save her life. She had lost too much blood. But I could turn her. She accepted my offer. When she woke as one of the night walkers, I learned that she was also a practitioner. Victoria was a gentle soul, and she could not stand the idea of harming others for her survival. I lost her after only ten days. But before she ended her own existence by meeting the sun, she left me a gift."

Regulus reached into the pocket of his black leather coat and withdrew a gold signet ring. "Daybreak approaches. In three hours, I will be forced underground, and I will not allow myself to be trapped in one of their cells again. This ring will allow me a short time to walk in the sun."

"What the bloody hell is 'a short time'?" Farren slid across the smooth leather and tucked herself in at Eli's side. "Ya' mean to tell me ya' brought us here, intendin' to fight with us, but knowin' ya'd be useless if the sun came up?"

Regulus narrowed his eyes at her in the rearview mirror, and despite how helpful he'd been, Eli didn't appreciate the indifference in his gaze. "The abilities of my kind are quite well known. Surely you were not so terribly preoccupied you failed to notice *the time?*"

Farren growled, low in her throat. A warning Eli feared meant she was close to losing control of her wolf.

"If I had intended to abandon you, I would not have brought the ring." A hint of emotion crept into the vampire's tone. Something Eli thought might even be regret. "This will allow me to sun walk until its magic has been depleted. The first time I had cause to put it on, the enchantments lasted hours. But in the decades since Victoria's passing, it has degraded."

"You'll be wise not to keep any more secrets from us,

vampire," Eli warned, surprised at the possessiveness and outright threat carried in his tone. Farren met his gaze, shock and arousal dilating her pupils. Rather than question him, she draped her hand over his thigh and leaned in to whisper in his ear.

"The full moon is but thirty minutes away. It'll have us both wantin' to rip apart anyone who comes between us by daybreak."

Despite his fear of what they'd find once they reached the castle—or perhaps because of it—Eli stole a moment with his mate, yanking her against him and ravaging her mouth. Her hands wandered until his dick stiffened under her touch. It wasn't until Regulus cleared his throat that either of them remembered where they were.

"Wolves," the vampire muttered as he took a sharp turn.

Eli missed her warmth as soon as Farren put space between them. The longer he spent with her, talking, kissing, fucking, the more he knew he wouldn't survive without her. Facing the Thirteen knowing he could easily lose her to their magic? It made the task even more daunting.

"Somethin' on yer mind, night walker?" Farren asked. "We were havin' a moment."

"I have been alive longer than the two of you can imagine. And as is the case for most vampires, I have spent the majority of that time alone. My progeny are scattered across the world, for I do not compel them to stay with me. These centuries have taught me many things, but I have forgotten much as well. Such as human emotions and their importance."

It was more of an apology than Eli had expected out of the creature, and, at his side, Farren nodded. "Right, then. I suppose we're all a mite tense."

"The Thirteen are cunning and cruel. They know what I am and how to cause me the greatest pain, and they will know the same about every one of you within minutes of crossing their wards. It is their way." Regulus turned the ring over in his long, elegant fingers. "The ring is no mystery to them."

Farren sank back against the rich leather seat. "Then are ya' sure it will even work? They could counter its magic without breakin' a sweat, yeah?"

The worry lines etched around his mate's lips riled something deep inside Eli. He'd cocked up the first casting so thoroughly to get them into this mess, and now he expected her—and the rest of the werewolves and elementals with them—to trust him. He had to find some way to redeem himself.

Before he'd done more than *decide* to lean forward and stick his head between the gap in the front seats, Regulus tensed like he'd expected the motion. "When Victoria enchanted the ring...do you remember the words she used?"

Regulus rolled his eyes. "I am a vampire. I remember *everything.*"

"There ya' go again," Farren muttered, and her exasperation brought a smile to curve Eli's lips. His mate was always so controlled, even when her temper got the better of her. But with him, there was softness, tenderness...affection. If they got out of this alive, he'd never stop telling her how much he loved every part of her.

"Tell me the words she used," Eli said as he returned his focus to the gold bauble in the vampire's palm. "If there's a chance I can restore the ring to its full power, then you'll be able to fight with us no matter how long it takes."

THE OLD CASTLE loomed against the starry sky. Lights blazed from several of the windows, and next to Farren, Eli shuddered. "Something about this place feels very...wrong," he said.

"You are sensing the Thirteen's collective power." Regulus pulled off the road and maneuvered the car between clumps of thick bushes and small trees. The other two cars—one with Ewan, Tierney, and Peter and the last with Cade, Liam, and Caitlin—followed, and the group huddled together next to a large cedar tree.

Eli broke away from the group, the ring in his hand, and closed his eyes, reciting the words Regulus had relayed to him. At first, nothing happened. Not even a tingle against his skin or a slight warmth in his fingers.

But as he chanted, a part of his mind started to wander. A sudden tug in the center of his chest shocked him, and he opened his eyes to see a beautiful garden surrounding him.

A woman, deathly pale, sad, and with eyes as red as blood stared at him. "You do not belong here."

"I seek only to protect the one who made you." Eli didn't know how he recognized Victoria, given that he'd never seen her before, but her connection to the ring was unmistakable.

"He still walks the night?" she asked.

"He does. He is a good man." Eli held out his hand. "Lend me some of your power, and I will do my best to ensure he sees another moon."

Victoria's small fingers brushed the ring, and as quickly as he'd been tugged into the past, he found himself back in Scotland, the gold pulsing with energy.

Approaching the rest of the group, he passed it to Regulus. "She cared for you. Deeply. And I believe she was sad to leave you."

The vampire stared at the ring, his eyes wide and an expression of deep longing and remorse crossing his features for a blink. "Thank you for bringing her back to me, even if only as a memory."

Farren wrapped an arm around Eli's waist. "Ya' did it?"

"I think so," he said. "I did *something*. I just hope it's enough."

Regulus tucked the ring into a pocket deep inside his coat and when he turned back to the group, all trace of emotion had vanished from his face. "As I explained on the flight," he began, "the dungeons are underground. If Mara is here, that is where you will find her. Eliziam, if your father lives, he could be on one of the other levels. He is a prisoner, yes, but the Thirteen know he will not try to escape, and I believe they keep him close to be able to serve them at their pleasure."

Farren stepped forward. "Cade, Liam, Peter, and Tierney will shift. As will I. Ewan, I want ya' to stay in yer human form as long as ya' can in case one of us needs to communicate somethin' to Eli, Caitlin, or Regulus. Take as many of these bastards out as ya' can."

The wolves nodded in turn and started stripping out of their clothing. Regulus buttoned his long leather coat, then rolled up the sleeves. Steel daggers were strapped to both of his arms, and he tested each of them, jerking his hand to release some sort of spring mechanism that drove the blade forward. "I am ready. We are agreed on our two groups?"

"Cade, Liam, Peter, and Caitlin will head for the dungeons," Farren said. "You, Eli, Tierney, and I will find the Thirteen. Ewan is to keep watch and move between the two groups as he can, but he'll stick with us unless he's called underground."

Eli took Farren's hand and drew her away from the rest of the group. He had to tell her now. "This is the most inappropriate conversation in the history of inappropriate conversations," he said as he gathered her in his arms. "I love you, Farren. When the moon rises, no matter where we are, no matter if we're still battling those bastards, whether we succeed or get our arses handed to us, I am your mate."

"Are ya' sure, *mo ghra?*" she asked. "I'm not a good bet. I'm a shite alpha. What if I'm rubbish at bein' yer mate as well?"

"You're not any of those things." He skimmed her cheek with a knuckle and cupped the back of her neck. "You are the most amazing, powerful, and brave person I have ever met. You have two packs that love you. One you lead and one who's chosen you to protect them knowing you *won't* fail."

Tears shone in Farren's gray eyes, and she pulled him down until she could brush her lips to his neck. A growl started in her throat, and she bit down, hard enough Eli had to stifle his yelp of surprise. The pain faded in an instant, replaced by pure, almost overwhelming pleasure.

"I just marked ya', Eli. Not the matin' bite. Not yet. We've a short time left. But a promise. If we live through this, ye're mine."

"Then let's make sure we survive. Because I won't lose you."

With one hard, passionate kiss, Eli released her and stepped back so his mate could shift into her wolf. He lost his breath when he caught sight of her eyes. They glowed, and in their depths he found more than determination. More than bravery. More than the raw power her gaze always held.

Now, they also held a confidence that had not been there before.

"You only need to accept your flaws. And hers."

Eli glanced at the vampire. Regulus's lips curved into something approaching a smile, and he nodded. "You have taken the biggest step," he said over the sound of cracking bones and muffled lupine whimpers. "Now, we see if the two of you are strong enough to complete the journey together."

CHAPTER TWENTY-FOUR

ELI

He felt it the moment they crossed the barrier. A burning pain deep inside him as the markings across his torso flared to life. He shot Regulus a look full of disdain.

"You couldn't have warned me how much it would hurt?"

The vampire shrugged. "I did not want to take the chance you would hesitate."

Eli growled, and at his side, Farren echoed the sound. Though he didn't understand most of the wolves' vocalizations, his mate's was clear. If Regulus was keeping any other secrets from them, she'd tear him apart.

He didn't think she could—not with how strong the night walker was rumored to be—but knowing he and Farren could still share emotions, even with her in wolf form, reassured him. Reaching down, he ruffled her fur, and the sound she made soothed his every nerve.

"I'm all right," he said when the worst of the agony had

passed. "I can go on."

They hadn't gone more than another two meters when a percussive force sent the group flying backwards. Liam and Tierney whimpered in pain, and Farren exchanged some odd vocalizations with Cade that Eli couldn't understand.

Ewan, still in his human form, got to his feet. "Movement. Northwest corner of the castle. Two of them," he explained.

"Leave them to me." Regulus moved so quickly, Eli saw only a black-clad blur. Two seconds later, screams echoed across the landscape. Fuck. He hoped Regulus knew what he was doing.

"You doubted me, practitioner?" The vampire wiped blood from his lips and snorted, already back at Eli's side. "They were novitiates. The Thirteen are apparently recruiting. Easy prey. But the next ones we face? They will not be."

Farren barked, and they split up.

Cade's group headed for the crimson-stained doorway Regulus had just cleared, while the vampire led the rest of them around the back of the castle to a heavy iron gate. Mists swirled beyond the bars, dark gray and seemingly with a life of their own.

Without so much as a grunt for his effort, Regulus ripped the gate from its hinges and tossed it a good half a kilometer. "Pathetic."

In the next breath—though did vampires actually breathe?— the night walker stumbled and fell to his knees.

"There is silver in the air," he managed before his eyes rolled back in his head and spasms started to shake his entire body. Farren barked a warning, and Ewan translated.

"Hold yer breath. All of ya.'" Hefting the vampire on his shoulder, the young wolf sprinted forward with Eli right behind him. Whatever they encountered next, Eli had to be ready for.

The mists cleared after another few seconds, and a plain wooden door came into view. Eli called a stiff breeze to dispel the last of the mists, and within a few seconds, Regulus groaned.

"Put me down, wolf." He braced his hand against the old, moss-covered stones. "I will be at full strength again before you can get that door open."

Ewan snorted and offered up his wrist. "Feed, bloodsucker. But if ya' take more than a few drops, I'm countin' on Farren to rip out yer throat."

Regulus wrinkled his nose. "I do not enjoy wolf blood." Despite his protest, he grabbed Ewan's hand and sank his teeth into the young man's arm. He pulled away two seconds later, and the wounds sealed themselves as Regulus licked his lips. "The taste of fur is unmistakable. Even when you are in this form."

"Ye're welcome," Ewan muttered.

Eli's magic started as a warmth in his chest, steadily growing hotter until it demanded to be let free. Regulus snapped the door knob into pieces while Eli called fire to his left hand and water to his right. At his side, Farren gave him an encouraging yip, and the door swung inwards.

Empty. They'd found a large kitchen, complete with half a dozen cauldrons set over flame right alongside what looked to be a brand new Viking gas range with twelve burners in glistening stainless steel. The entire space was a mix of the old world and the new. An espresso machine on the counter, but behind it, jars containing pieces of animals Eli wanted to know nothing about.

"Feckin' loons," Ewan muttered.

"Silence." Regulus held up his hand and pointed down the hall to the left. "Four. At least. I will take out as many as I can, but be ready, practitioner." Taking off with his blinding fast speed, the vampire disappeared, and the sounds that came from the next room chilled Eli to the bone.

CAITLIN

The stench of blood turned her stomach, but Caitlin called upon her air to clear the scent from her nose as soon as they'd crossed the threshold. Cade and Liam kept her between them, with Peter bringing up the rear, and she was damn glad she'd spent so much time with the two of them in wolf form over the past few months. She understood them easily now, unless they got overly excited and started yipping and barking so quickly, they talked over one another.

Regulus had drawn them a map of the castle. The dungeons were in the northwest corner, down a long, curving set of stone stairs. He hadn't been conscious when the practitioners had brought him to this place, but believed magic hid the door from the outside.

Caitlin reached into her cross-body bag and found the smoky quartz crystal by touch alone. Tracing several sigils in the air, she sent her element flowing out in all directions. Though the room, which looked to be some sort of common room with a large television on one wall and a pool table in the center, was pristine, her casting stirred whatever dust it could find and drew it towards the magic.

A bookcase? Could the Thirteen have used a more cliche spell?

She huffed, and Cade bounded for the wooden shelves that appeared to hold ancient tomes with Latin titles in gold foil along their spines. His wolf stopped only an inch away, sniffed, and swore under his breath. At least, that's what Caitlin had always thought that sound meant.

Before she could take another step closer, Cade jumped and disappeared. Liam growled until Cade's head popped back out in the middle of a row of books.

"Feckin' hell. That's...disturbing," Caitlin whispered.

One by one, they all passed through the magic, and Caitlin shivered as its chill raised the hair on her arms. It felt *wrong* on so many levels, but if they had a chance to free Mara, there wasn't anything she wouldn't do.

Torches provided the only light here, as if the practitioners wanted any prisoner to understand that the old ways were often the best. They descended for what felt like forever, and had to be at least two standard flights of stairs.

At the bottom, Cade rounded the corner first and growled, *"Danger!"*

A blast of light and power exploded off one of the rough-hewn stone walls, and Cade's wolf whimpered and leapt back, a patch of fur at his shoulder smoking.

Caitlin used a bit of her air to cool the burn and sent out a locator charm. She held up three fingers, then dropped to one knee and took Liam's muzzle between her hands. "I can't sense Mara," she whispered in his ear. "Only magic."

Gesturing to the wolves, she indicated roughly where she thought each practitioner was, then conjured a thick bank of fog and sent it racing around the corner.

The wolves followed, snarls and growls echoing off the walls. Sweet, coppery blood was all she could smell, and finally, Caitlin yelled, "Now!"

Her next charm not only wiped away the fog, but stole all the air from the space. The wolves had been prepared, but the practitioners—the two of them left alive—clawed at their throats as they fought to draw breath.

Cade's jaws closed over a short, squat man's throat, and he ripped into the practitioner's jugular. A spray of blood painted the wolf's cheek, but he didn't seem to care.

She couldn't keep the charm active any longer or they'd all pass out, and air returned with a *whoosh* just as the last practitioner sent her mate flying away from her down the corridor. Liam's body hit metal, and Caitlin screamed.

"That's my mate, ya' fuckin' piece of shite!"

The compulsion charm came to her and flowed from her lips

both easy and painful in equal measure. So many times, Fergus had used the same sort of charm on her, and she hated him for it, even after his death at her hand.

After she'd used one on Liam and the rest of the pack months ago, she'd vowed to never attempt one again. But if they couldn't make one of the practitioners talk, they might never find Mara.

The woman, whose blond hair was shorn close to her scalp, looked to be around Caitlin's age until she caught sight of those dark purple eyes. A century or more of wisdom swirled in their depths.

Thank God the practitioner couldn't speak. If she'd been able, Caitlin was certain they'd all be dead by now. Or locked in one of the cells lining the passageway.

The earth shook violently enough Caitlin almost lost her hold on the charm. Eli. Whatever they were battling above ground could kill everyone below if they didn't hurry.

"Liam! Are ya' hurt?" Caitlin called out. Her mate growled, the sound weaker than she liked, but he limped out of the darkness and snarled as he passed the charmed woman.

All three wolves stood in front of the witch, and Caitlin twisted the compulsion charm to her will. "You will answer my questions and *only* my questions. If you try to say anythin' else, yer words will choke ya'. Where is Mara?"

"Not...here." Veins in the practitioner's neck strained with each word.

"Ya' consider that an answer? Hardly. Where is she? Answer or I'll leave ya' with no air to breathe at all."

"Hidden."

This woman was worse than Paddy, and the wolves were losing patience quickly. Cade snapped at her, tearing into her thigh. With a grunt, the witch collapsed to the ground and pressed her hands to the wound to try to stop the bleeding.

"Take us to her. Or I won't be responsible for what he does

to ya' next."

"I cannot."

They were going to fail. Caitlin's heart ached for Mara. For the woman she considered a sister, for the baby, and for Cade. She couldn't tighten the charm any more or she'd kill the woman, but if they didn't get an answer, Cade would do the job for her.

If she could only find a question the woman couldn't fail to answer. "How do we find her?"

"The voice of one who cannot speak and the sight of one who has never seen will find the blood of the stone. Without those, you are doomed to fail, and the elemental will be ours forever."

Cade shifted back into his human form, grabbed the practitioner by the throat, and slammed her into the wall. "You have my mate and my unborn child, you piece of shit. If you think for one fucking minute I'm not going to kill every practitioner on this entire goddamned planet to get her back, you're sorely mistaken. Starting with you."

"I am already dead." The practitioner started to choke, and though Caitlin dropped the compulsion charm, the woman continued to shake and flail.

"It's not me!" Caitlin cried when Cade shot her a lethal glare.

"No. Of course not, elemental," came a man's voice from behind Caitlin. "I took Kalitha's life. She served her purpose."

They all whirled around. Cade dropped the dead practitioner and snarled at the man with his hands glowing white hot.

"What. Purpose?" he growled.

"Distraction and diversion," the man said. "And once I kill the alpha wolf and break the mating bond, our success will be assured. The elemental and her child are the key to all."

The practitioner sent the brilliantly white light hurtling towards the four of them, and blinded, Caitlin screamed as chaos surrounded her.

CHAPTER TWENTY-FIVE

FARREN

Tierney bounded into the room at Farren's side with Eli and Ewan behind them. Next to the window, Regulus sunk his fangs into a tall man's neck, and the magic swirling around his victim's hands dimmed as the vampire fed.

Three other practitioners, including the woman from the beach, advanced on the wolves. "I knew you would come," she said, her voice strangely compelling.

Farren snarled and sprang for the practitioner, her front paws catching the woman in the chest and driving her to the stone floor. Tierney bounded for a second woman, while Eli sent a burst of flame towards the last practitioner standing.

Heavy, velvet draperies caught fire, and Regulus cried out as his coat started to burn. Farren whined, and Ewan directed Eli to douse the vampire with a wave of water. Fire, silver, and sunlight were the easiest ways to kill one of the night walkers, and they needed Regulus if they were going to survive this.

"I am Glenna, you feral bitch," the practitioner under

Farren's massive paws bit out. "And you are going to die tonight. With the power from the elemental and her child, we will be able to turn your mate into the most powerful weapon the world has ever seen!"

Oh, *hell* no. Farren's jaws were only a breath away from Glenna's throat when the woman whispered a string of words in some ancient Scottish tongue.

The world went soft and quiet, and Farren toppled over with a faint whimper. Why couldn't she move? Her nose twitched, the scent of magic cloying, but her legs wouldn't obey her commands, and her tongue lolled out of her mouth.

"Farren!" Eli cried. He blasted Glenna with a strong gale, sending the practitioner tumbling into an old, dark wood table, and knelt at Farren's side. "Fight, *preciosa*, please."

She was trying. God, she was trying with everything she had. Ewan slumped over a leather sofa. Tierney huddled in a corner, and even Regulus appeared frozen, his hand tucked into the pocket of his coat.

"Isla, he is all yours," Glenna said, and Farren whined, but her warning came too late.

Isla appeared out of nowhere and pressed a knife to Eli's throat. "Stand up slowly, Eliziam. Fight me, and your mate dies painfully. Do as I say, and I will make her death quick."

Before Farren could make another sound, someone approached from behind her and snapped a tight, thick collar around her neck. The metal choked her, and she was dragged backwards away from Eli.

"Prepare to meet the sun, nightwalker," Glenna hissed, and with a flick of her hand, destroyed the entire outside wall of the large space Farren thought might be a dining room.

The sun's first light poured in, and Regulus screamed. Smoke rose from his skin, from the hand he'd stretched towards Tierney. The first flame licked up his neck, and he fell to his knees.

Another incomprehensible phrase, and whatever spell had been binding them fell away. But it was too late. Tierney had been leashed and fitted with a muzzle, held by a young man with a scar down his right cheek, a tall bloke with blazing purple eyes snapped Ewan's neck before the boy could even move, and blood welled in a thin line across Eli's throat.

No. Not again. I failed them. All of them.

Farren howled, the mournful sound echoing off the remaining walls. Regulus's coat was burning now, and he rocked back and forth as he screamed in agony.

In that moment, the moon rose, and every muscle in Farren's lithe, lupine body screamed for her mate. She had to get to him. Had to touch him, save him, just be *near* him. But as she strained against the collar and leash, a needle pierced her pelt, and she froze..

"Da'." The single, hoarse word from Eli silenced Farren in an instant. Her mate was staring just over her shoulder. At the man holding the leash. And the needle. She tried to turn her head and caught a glimpse of Paulo Ruiz. His eyes—as Regulus had said—were empty. Almost. Was that...a tear shining in one of them? His thumb hovered just above the syringe plunger.

"He has not been your father in twenty years, Eliziam," Glenna said, her voice taunting and almost...gleeful. "He is ours now. As you soon will be. The syringe contains a concentrated dose of wolfsbane. Even in miniscule amounts, it can kill a human or a werewolf, but in that volume? Your wolf's heart will stop seconds after I command my little puppet to depress the plunger. Blair? Remove Eliziam's shirt."

Farren cared little that she might be about to die. If she could save Eli, her entire life would have meaning.

A slight woman—barely more than a girl—appeared just in front of Eli.

What the hell? Had she...teleported? That would explain how they got Mara out of my house so easily.

Blair pulled an athame from a leather holster at her side and sliced down the front of Eli's Henley. With precise cuts, she removed the entire garment then trailed the tip of the blade down the center of Eli's chest.

"No. You will not put another mark on my mate!" She doubted anyone but Tierney could understand her, and her howls earned her a hard jerk on the chain, but Farren had to find a way to stop these bastards from hurting him.

The girl started chanting, and Eli dropped his arms, his eyes wide and panic flooding the green depths. His mouth opened and closed several times, like he was desperate to tell Farren *something,* but no sound escaped his throat.

Flashing a brief smile in Farren's direction, Blair took hold of Eli's right hand, raised the athame high over her head, and then plunged it through his palm.

"I do not think you will be performing another casting for some time," Glenna said with a chuckle. "Blair, the other one, please."

Eli's father hissed behind Farren, and the tip of the syringe popped free from her pelt. He stroked Farren's fur with a single finger, and sorrow flowed through the touch, along with something else. The barest hint of hope mixed with desperation.

The young practitioner dropped Eli's right hand and reached for his left. Farren whined like she couldn't stand to watch and turned to look at Paulo. His eyes flicked to his side, then hers. Right where Fergus's scar would forever remind her how close she came to death.

The mark was a sigil of control. One the practitioners used to keep their victims in line.

Paulo gave Farren a tiny nod. If she failed, she'd not only lose her life, but Eli's as well. And she doubted he'd *ever* forgive her for what she was about to do. The moon was full. A bite now… she'd either kill Paulo or…

I have no choice.

For the briefest of seconds, she held her mate's gaze. Then, just as Blair took his left hand, Farren snarled and sank her jaws into Paulo's side.

ELI

Pain overrode all rational thought. The fingers of his right hand spasmed uncontrollably, and the kid—Blair, he thought—had a hold of his left now. The symbols branded across his skin flared to life, and he swore they were *yelling* at him. Begging him to fight. But without the use of his voice or his hands, he was powerless.

Across the room, his mate was about to die at *his father's hand.* Paulo didn't recognize him, hadn't even reacted when Eli had called him "da'." The knife to his throat burned, and he was losing blood too quickly. Had Isla nicked his carotid? No. He'd be dead already?

Farren snarled, and the leash flew from his father's hand as she whirled around and tore a chunk of flesh from Paulo's side. He screamed, blood soaking into his gray tunic, and sank to his knees.

His mate had *killed* his father. No. Not his father. The Thirteen's slave. Farren bounded towards him, the leash trailing behind her as she tackled Blair and sent the young girl arse over tea kettle. But Isla still had the knife pressed to Eli's throat.

Until Regulus, whose coat was still smoldering, rose in one smooth motion. He lifted his left hand, and Eli sucked in a sharp breath. Gold—melted gold—wound around his burned fingers like a delicate lattice. His sharp fangs glistened in the sun, but he didn't seem to care. He was on Isla in under two seconds, wrenching the knife from her grasp and ripping out her throat.

Tierney kicked the practitioner holding him, and he and

Farren headed straight for Glenna. She flung a spell at them, but Tierney jumped in front of Farren. Blue sparks singed his fur, and he hit the ground, his legs twitching and his eyes closed.

Farren clamped down on Glenna's arm with her massive jaws and ripped her hand clean off. The practitioner screamed and pulled a blade from her pocket, but Farren dodged the strike easily.

Eli, on his knees now, called on the power of earth. The entire building started to shake, and he let his rage take over. He'd end every single fucking one of the practitioners for taking his parents from him.

The Trinity Knot over his heart throbbed, and he focused all of his power on his uninjured left hand. If he could become spirit—or call it somehow—he could destroy every practitioner in this castle without breaking a sweat.

The power built, slowly at first, then picking up speed like a boulder rolling down a mountain. Suddenly, he couldn't control it.

"Farren!" he screamed, unable to move or let go of the over-abundance of magical energy. It was going to kill him if he couldn't direct it somewhere.

His mate lifted her massive head, and in her gray eyes, he found a measure of hope. She barked once and jerked her snout towards his father's body.

Eli didn't want to look. He'd ached for his parents—for one more hour, one more minute with them—for twenty years. And before he'd even had the chance to see his father acknowledge who he was, Farren had killed him.

The snarl shocked him, and he whipped his head around. The blood-stained gray tunic was in shreds, and a rail-thin wolf, his fur as dark as midnight, stood over the ruined garments.

"Da'?" he croaked.

The wolf—who had to be his father—bounded for Glenna, and the sound of cracking bones and Farren's whimpers made it hard to breathe. The power was still churning inside him, begging to be freed, but he couldn't let go. If he did, he'd destroy half the continent. Or at least, that's how it felt.

"Eli! Look at me." Farren staggered to her feet, gloriously naked and beautiful in her human form. Regulus was somewhere behind him, tearing into anyone who dared enter the room. Tierney had freed himself from the muzzle and was now working with Eli's father to rip Glenna to shreds.

His mate's hands stroked down his arms, and she took his uninjured hand and held it to her breast. Under his palm, he felt the Tree of Life pendant. "Send the power into the necklace, luv."

"The casting...will kill you," he whispered.

"You must be willing to sacrifice all that you are."

The vampire's words came back to him, and he held Farren's gaze.

"I'm not afraid, Eli. Whatever happens, this is what I want." She leaned in and pressed her lips to his. "Let me do this, *mo ghra*. Trust me, and I'll trust you."

In that moment, Eli felt all the broken pieces in his mate's soul mend. The guilt she carried over Colin, Brian, and Abagail melted away. There was no place for that emotion any longer. She felt only love for him, and he for her.

"I'm yers, Eliziam Escobar Ruiz Colón. And I do not intend to lose ya'. Do it. Right feckin' now."

<hr>

FARREN

Fear churned in her mate's eyes. How could she make him understand? "I love ya', Eli. I'll always love ya'. In this life and the next." She cupped his cheek and brushed her lips to his. The power thrumming through him…she could taste it, bitter yet sweet on her tongue.

"Ya' won't kill me, luv. Ya' have power no one has ever seen before, and I believe ya' can control it."

Time slowed to a near standstill. To her left, Regulus finished draining Isla and released her lifeless body. To her right, Paulo and Tierney stood over the remaining pieces of Glenna. Farren wasn't sure what Cade, Liam, Caitlin, and Peter had found, and she mourned Ewan's death, the hole in her heart growing larger by the minute with all the pack members she'd lost.

But she didn't have to lose Eli.

Farren curled her mate's fingers around the pendant. "Trust me. I've never been more certain of anything in my entire life."

She felt it the second he let go. Not even her first shift could compare to the agony of absorbing that much power. The tree of life burned and sizzled against her skin, and Farren screamed. The castle walls shook, bits of plaster and stone falling all around them.

Regulus took off in a blur of motion, carrying Paulo and Tierney—both still in wolf form—through the destroyed window, then returning for Ewan's body.

"I will retrieve the others," he shouted. "Do not linger!"

The others. Cade. Liam. Caitlin. Peter. Mara.

God, she hoped Mara was with them.

She and Eli stood rooted, connected, and unable to move. His guilt and pain were a bitter taste in her mouth, and she softened her gaze, the only motion she seemed capable of.

"You have nothing to regret, Eli. Nothing. I'm alive. Yer father is alive. You stopped a feckin' vampire from burning to death in the sun."

If only he could hear her. Or…could he? A tear glistened in the corner of his eye, and Farren strained to raise her hand and wipe it away.

The contact seemed to free him from the magic holding him

prisoner, and he grabbed her, hauling her naked body up and tossing her over his shoulder. Regulus passed them twice, carrying a wolf and a human each time.

Farren couldn't tell if Mara was one of the humans, but she held onto Eli like her life depended on it. And then she felt the oddest sensation. Like…they were floating. She saw nothing but a blur, and they moved from the half-destroyed room to the grass in the blink of an eye. As soon as Farren scented the fresh morning air, her heart stopped pounding half out of her chest.

Her bare feet touched damp grass, and Eli's hands framed her face. His kiss? She'd never been kissed like that before, and fuck. She wanted it again. Every day for the rest of her life.

The pendant around her neck still burned, and she whimpered, the sound muffled by his lips. But her mate would always hear her. He drew back, curled his fingers around the pendant, and flung his mangled hand in the direction of the castle.

"Is everyone out?" he shouted, and Regulus confirmed the castle was empty of all but practitioners.

Eli closed his eyes, and the most beautiful rays of light shot out from each one of his fingers.

The light curled around the castle walls like ribbons, and after what had to be no more than a minute, shrank down to a single pinprick, taking the entire castle with it.

The sudden absence of power left Farren hollow, and Eli clearly felt its loss as well. Still holding on to one another, they fell to the ground, a tangle of arms and legs, and though Farren feared they'd lost so much more than they'd bargained for, she was with her mate.

EPILOGUE

FARREN

She wasn't sure how she'd gotten into a car. Or who'd draped a blanket over her. All she knew was that she and Eli were together.

"What...happened?" she managed, though she couldn't quite open her eyes.

Eli groaned, clearly as addled as she was.

From the front seat, Regulus cleared his throat. Even with that simple action, he managed to affect an air of superiority. But when he spoke, awe infused his tone.

"There were six full-fledged members of the Thirteen in that house. Five are dead. One escaped. The rest were apprentices and novitiates. Still powerful, but not unbeatable. The five, however...should have ended us all."

Farren forced her eyes open to slits to find bright sunlight streaming through the front windshield. "How are you driving?"

Regulus held up his hand. A ribbon of gold wound around fingers that would never be anything but burned again. "The fire should have killed me. However, I had just touched the ring Eliziam spelled for me. The heat destroyed it, but the power...that has not faded. At least not yet. I can walk in the sun for the first time in almost three hundred years without fear."

"What about...Paulo?" Farren asked.

"The wolf born of Eliziam's father ran as I was attempting to rouse the male alpha and his beta. But he is alive. He fought valiantly, and I dare say, some of the guilt he carried for years has been assuaged."

"I need...to find...him..." Eli whispered.

"He will find you, practitioner. Of that I am certain." Regulus banked the car into a gentle turn, and after another few minutes, eased it to a stop. "This is one of my homes. It is warded, so you will be safe here. As will my newest progeny."

Farren pushed up on an elbow. "Your newest...?"

Regulus was out of the car and had the back door open before Farren registered he'd even moved. Taking a knee, he stared down at his burned hand. "Eliziam did for me what no creature in centuries has been able to. My life debt is no longer simply to his father. It is to him and to you as well. Vampires... we can invade others' minds, Farren Denair. I saw your guilt over the deaths of your pack members before we left Ireland. When I felt the sunlight hit my face and I did not turn to dust, I knew I could not let you suffer another loss." He stepped back as she found enough strength to get to her feet and then help Eli join her.

Her mate held on to her, and they supported one another. They were underground now, in a massive garage with a dozen vehicles, and Regulus opened the boot and gestured for them to join him.

Ewan lay wrapped in a blanket, his face deathly pale. "I have never turned a werewolf before. He may well decide he wishes to meet the sun as my Victoria did, but if that is what he wishes,

I will ensure the end to his existence is painless. I give you my vow."

The vampire placed his hand over his heart, and Farren's eyes burned with tears she couldn't let fall. She'd never trusted a vampire. Never thought any were worthy of her trust. Until now. The mating wouldn't let her hug Regulus. No. She wouldn't touch another man who wasn't her mate ever again unless she had to. But she held his blood-red gaze. "You do not owe me a feckin' thing, night walker. Ya' repaid yer debt a hundred times over, and I thank ya' for it."

THE MOON SET, and she and Eli had barely moved after Regulus had shown them to a suite on the second floor of the home. He had bedrooms for everyone, but Cade, who was inconsolable after they'd failed to find Mara, was currently raging below ground where he could punch the stone walls to his heart's content.

Liam had sent Peter back to Farren's to retrieve Diedre's book and a few bags of essentials, but he and Caitlin had taken a room at the end of the hall. Tierney was bunking underground next to the concrete room Cade had locked himself in, and Farren had no idea where Ewan was transitioning.

She wished she could help the young man through what would certainly be the most traumatic experience of his life, but her mate needed her, and she knew less than nothing about a vampire's making.

Regulus assured her that Ewan would be well cared for, and she believed him.

"Farrrrrrr....ennnn." Eli's groan drew her focus, and she looked into his tired, green eyes. "My father..."

"He's in the wind, Eli. But we will find him. He's free from the Thirteen's control. That I can promise you."

Eli reached for her, and when she rolled on top of him, something she'd never known had been out of sorts settled deep inside of her. "We survived," he said.

"We did. But Mara wasn't there."

Her mate's entire body stiffened. "Fuck me."

Farren brushed a lock of hair off his forehead. "The practitioner Caitlin charmed gave us this. 'The voice of one who cannot speak and the sight of one who has never seen will find the blood of the stone. Without those, you are doomed to fail, and the elemental will be ours forever.'"

"What the hell does that mean?" Eli asked.

"No feckin' clue. But it's somethin'. If there's a divine bein' up there guidin' us, she'll send Paddy here right quick, and perhaps he'll have an idea. Cade's lost himself to madness, and Liam…he can hardly stand it."

Farren skimmed her lips over Eli's, and the connection between the two of them soothed her in ways she'd never known she'd needed.

"We need to find him. Now," Eli said, but as he tried to sit up, his eyes rolled back in his head.

"Easy now, luv. The practitioner who almost killed Caitlin, Liam, Cade, and Peter wanted to break the matin' bond between Cade and Mara. He claimed that would ensure their success. He failed, so it's likely Mara's still alive. And he mentioned the baby. I don't think they plan on killin' Mara until the pup is born." Farren skimmed the back of her hand over Eli's cheek. "When the sun sets—" she glanced over at the clock on the nightstand, "—in four hours, we'll have a pack meetin' and figure out what to do next. Until then…"

Eli wrapped his arms around her. "I love you, Farren. I want to seal the mating. I don't want to be parted from you ever again."

Despite the stress and strain, the worry the whole house carried for Mara, the uncertainty of not knowing where Paulo was or whether Ewan would accept his new existence, Farren let herself smile. At least one part of her life made sense. Her love for her mate.

THANK you for reading *A Shift in the Earth*. Here's the part where I beg for your forgiveness over ending this book with a cliffhanger.

I really **hate** writing cliffhangers. I don't like doing it for me or for you. But, I can promise you that *A Shift in Fire*, the final book in the Elemental Shifter series, is complete and will be released on March 23, 2021.

So you won't have to wait long for the thrilling conclusion.

If you can spare just a few moments, I'd love it if you'd leave a review for *A Shift in the Earth*. Reviews don't have to be long or recap the book in any way. Just leave a sentence or two about how this book made you **feel**. Reviews really do help your favorite authors sell more books.

Plus, they're like hugs. And we could all use more hugs right now.

Love,
Patricia

ABOUT THE AUTHOR

I've always made up stories. Sometimes I even acted them out. I probably shouldn't admit that my childhood best friend and I used to run around the backyard pretending to fly in our Invisible Jet and rescue Steve Trevor. Oops.

Now that I'm too old to spin around in circles with felt magic bracelets on my wrists, I put "pen to paper" instead. Figuratively, at least. Fingers to keyboard is more accurate.

Outside of my writing, I'm a professional editor, a software geek, a singer (in the shower only), and a runner. I love red wine, scotch (neat, please), and cider. Seattle is my home, and I share an old house with my husband and cats.

I'm on my fourth—fifth?—rewatching of the modern *Doctor Who*, and I think one particular quote from that show sums up my entire life.

"We're all stories, in the end. Make it a good one, eh?" — *The Eleventh Doctor, Doctor Who*

I hope your story is brilliant.

You can reach me all over the web...
patriciadeddy.com
patricia@patriciadeddy.com

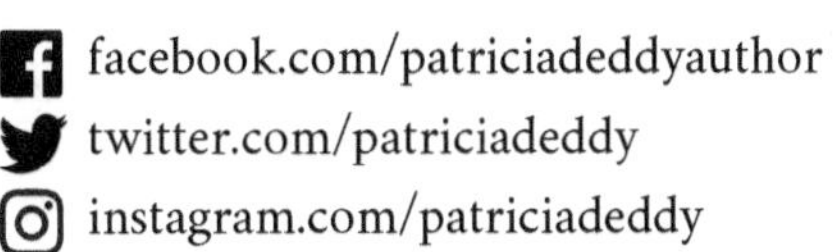
facebook.com/patriciadeddyauthor
twitter.com/patriciadeddy
instagram.com/patriciadeddy

Forever Kept

Immortal Hunter

Wicked Omens

Storm of Sin

ELEMENTAL SHIFTER

Hot werewolves and strong, powerful elementals. What's not to love?

A Shift in the Water

A Shift in the Air

A Shift in the Earth

A Shift in Fire

BY THE FATES

Check out the **COMPLETE** By the Fates series if you love dark and steamy tales of witches, devils, and an epic battle between good and evil.

By the Fates, Freed

Destined: A By the Fates Story

By the Fates, Fought

By the Fates, Fulfilled

IN BLOOD

If you love hot Italian vampires and and a human who can hold her own against beings far stronger, then the In Blood series is for you.

Secrets in Blood

Revelations in Blood

HOLIDAYS AND HEROES

Beauty isn't only skin deep and not all scars heal. Come swoon over sexy vets and the men and women who love them.

Mistletoe and Mochas

Love and Libations

RESTRAINED

Do you like to be tied up? Or read about characters who do? Enjoy a **COMPLETE** fresh BDSM series that will leave you begging for more.

In His Silks

Christmas Silks

All Tied Up For New Year's

In His Collar